Seven Little Australians

BY ETHEL TURNER

ANGUS
& ROBERTSON

An imprint of HarperCollins*Publishers*

To my Mother

AN ANGUS & ROBERTSON BOOK
An imprint of HarperCollinsPublishers

First published in Australia in 1894
This paperback edition first published in
Australia by Angus & Robertson Publishers in 1989
Reprinted 1989, 1990, 1991
CollinsAngus&Robertson Publishers Pty Limited (ACN 009 913 517)
A division of HarperCollinsPublishers (Australia) Pty Limited
4 Eden Park, 31 Waterloo Road, North Ryde, NSW 2113, Australia

William Collins Publishers Ltd
31 View Road, Glenfield, Auckland 10, New Zealand

HarperCollinsPublishers Limited
77-85 Fulham Palace Road, London W6 8JB, United Kingdom

National Library of Australia
Cataloguing-in-Publication data:

Turner, Ethel, 1872-1958.
  Seven little Australians.

  ISBN 0 207 17337 0
  I. Title.

A823'.2.

Cover illustration by Margaret Power and Sandra Laroche
Printed in Australia by Griffin Press Limited

 9   8   7   6   5   4
95 94 93 92 91

Contents

CHAPTER 1
Chiefly Descriptive 7

CHAPTER 2
Fowl for Dinner 14

CHAPTER 3
Virtue Not Always Rewarded 20

CHAPTER 4
The General Sees Active Service 35

CHAPTER 5
"Next Monday Morning" 49

CHAPTER 6
The Sweetness of Sweet Sixteen 55

CHAPTER 7
"What Say You to Falling in Love?" 63

CHAPTER 8
A Catapult and a Catastrophe 77

CHAPTER 9
Consequences 85

CHAPTER 10
Bunty in the Light of a Hero 89

CHAPTER 11
The Truant 102

CHAPTER 12
Swish, Swish! 110

CHAPTER 13
Uninvited Guests 119

CHAPTER 14
The Squatter's Invitation 128

CHAPTER 15
Three Hundred Miles in the Train 135

CHAPTER 16
Yarrahappini 145

CHAPTER 17
Cattle-Drafting at Yarrahappini 153

CHAPTER 18
The Picnic at Krangi-Bahtoo 160

CHAPTER 19
A Pale-Blue Hair Ribbon 168

CHAPTER 20
Little Judy 177

CHAPTER 21
When the Sun Went Down 183

CHAPTER 22
And Last 188

CHAPTER 1

Chiefly Descriptive

BEFORE YOU FAIRLY START this story I should like to give you just a word of warning.

If you imagine you are going to read of model children, with perhaps a naughtily inclined one to point a moral, you had better lay down the book immediately and betake yourself to *Sandford and Merton,* or similar standard juvenile works. Not one of the seven is really good, for the very excellent reason that Australian children never are.

In England, and America, and Africa, and Asia, the little folks may be paragons of virtue, I know little about them.

But in Australia a model child is—I say it not without thankfulness—an unknown quantity.

It may be that the miasmas of naughtiness develop best in the sunny brilliancy of our atmosphere. It may be that the land and the people are young-hearted together, and the children's spirits not crushed and saddened by the shadow of long years' sorrowful history.

There is a lurking sparkle of joyousness and rebellion and mischief in nature here, and therefore in children.

7

Often the light grows dull and the bright colouring fades to neutral tints in the dust and heat of the day. But when it survives play-days and school-days, circumstances alone determine whether the electric sparkle shall go to play will-o'-the-wisp with the larrikin type, or warm the breasts of the spirited, single-hearted, loyal ones who alone can " advance Australia."

Enough of such talk. Let me tell you about my seven select spirits. They are having nursery tea at the present moment with a minimum of comfort and a maximum of noise, so if you can bear a deafening babel of voices and an unmusical clitter-clatter of crockery I will take you inside the room and introduce them to you.

Nursery tea is more an English institution than an Australian one; there is a kind of *bon camaraderie* feeling between parents and young folks here, and an utter absence of veneration on the part of the latter. So even in the most wealthy families it seldom happens that the parents dine in solemn state alone, while the children are having a simple tea in another room: they all assemble around the same board, and the young ones partake of the same dishes, and sustain their parts in the conversation right nobly.

But, given a very particular and rather irritable father, and seven children with excellent lungs and tireless tongues, what could you do but give them separate rooms to take their meals in?

Captain Woolcot, the father, in addition to this division, had had thick felt put over the swing door upstairs, but the noise used to float down to the

8

dining-room in a cheerful, unconcerned manner despite it.

It was a nursery without a nurse, too, so that partly accounted for it. Meg, the eldest, was only sixteen, and could not be expected to be much of a disciplinarian, and the slatternly but good-natured girl, who was supposed to combine the duties of nursery-maid and housemaid, had so much to do in her second capacity that the first suffered considerably. She used to lay the nursery meals when none of the little girls could be found to help her, and bundle on the clothes of the two youngest in the morning, but beyond that the seven had to manage for themselves.

The mother? you ask.

Oh, she was only twenty—just a lovely, laughing-faced girl, whom they all adored, and who was very little steadier and very little more of a housekeeper than Meg. Only the youngest of the brood was hers, but she seemed just as fond of the other six as of it, and treated it more as if it were a very entertaining kitten than a real live baby, and her very own.

Indeed at Misrule—that is the name their house always went by, though I believe there was a different one painted above the balcony—that baby seemed a gigantic joke to everyone. The Captain generally laughed when he saw it, tossed it in the air, and then asked someone to take it quickly.

The children dragged it all over the country with them, dropped it countless times, forgot its pelisse on wet days, muffled it up when it was hot, gave it the most astounding things to eat, and yet it was the

9

healthiest, prettiest, and most sunshiny baby that ever sucked a wee fat thumb.

It was never called "Baby," either; that was the special name of the next youngest. Captain Woolcot had said, "Hello, is this the General?" when the little, red, staring-eyed morsel had been put into his arms, and the name had come into daily use, though I believe at the christening service the curate did say something about Francis Rupert Burnand Woolcot.

Baby was four, and was a little soft fat thing with pretty cuddlesome ways, great smiling eyes, and lips very kissable when they were free from jam.

She had a weakness, however, for making the General cry, or she would have been really almost a model child. Innumerable times she had been found pressing its poor little chest to make it "squeak," and even pinching its tiny arms, or pulling its innocent nose, just for the strange pleasure of hearing the yells of despair it instantly set up. Captain Woolcot ascribed the peculiar tendency to the fact that the child had once had a dropsical-looking woolly lamb, from which the utmost pressure would only elicit the faintest possible squeak: he said it was only natural that now she had something so amenable to squeezing she should want to utilize it.

Bunty was six, and was fat and very lazy. He hated scouting at cricket, he loathed the very name of a paper-chase, and as for running an errand, why, before anyone could finish saying something was wanted he would have utterly disappeared. He was rather small for his age, and I don't think had ever been seen with a clean face. Even at church, though the immediate front turned to the minister might be passable, the people in the next pew had always an uninterrupted view of the black rim where washing operations had left off.

The next on the list—I am going from youngest to oldest, you see—was the "show" Woolcot, as Pip, the eldest boy, used to say. You have seen those exquisite child-angel faces on Raphael Tuck's Christmas cards? I think the artist must just have dreamed of Nell, and then reproduced the vision imperfectly. She was ten, and had a little fairy-like figure, gold hair clustering in wonderful waves and curls around her face, soft hazel eyes, and a little rosebud of a mouth. She was not conceited either, her family took care of that—Pip would have nipped such a weakness very sternly in its earliest bud; but in some way if there was a pretty ribbon to spare, or a breadth of bright material just enough for one little frock, it fell as a matter of course to her.

Judy was only three years older, but was the greatest contrast imaginable. Nellie used to move rather slowly about, and would have made a picture in any attitude. Judy, I think, was never seen to walk, and seldom looked picturesque. If she did not dash madly to the place she wished to get to, she would progress by a series of jumps, bounds, and odd little skips. She was very thin, as people generally are who have quicksilver instead of blood in their veins; she had a small, eager, freckled face, with very bright dark eyes, a small, determined mouth, and a mane of untidy, curly dark hair that was the trial of her life.

11

Without doubt she was the worst of the seven, probably because she was the cleverest. Her brilliant inventive powers plunged them all into ceaseless scrapes, and though she often bore the brunt of the blame with equanimity, they used to turn round, not infrequently, and upbraid her for suggesting the mischief. She had been christened " Helen," which in no way accounts for " Judy," but then nicknames are rather unaccountable things sometimes, are they not? Bunty said it was because she was always popping and jerking herself about like the celebrated wife of Punch, and there really is something in that. Her other name, " Fizz," is easier to understand; Pip used to say he never yet had seen the ginger ale that effervesced and bubbled and made the noise that Judy did.

I haven't introduced you to Pip yet, have I? He was a little like Judy, only handsomer and taller, and he was fourteen, and had as good an opinion of himself and as poor a one of girls as boys of that age generally have.

Meg was the eldest of the family, and had a long, fair plait that Bunty used to delight in pulling, a sweet, rather dreamy face, and a powdering of pretty freckles that occasioned her much tribulation of spirit.

It was generally believed in the family that she wrote poetry and stories, and even kept a diary, but no one had ever seen a vestige of her papers, she kept them so carefully locked up in her old tin hat-box. Their father, had you asked them, they would all have replied with considerable pride, was " a military man," and much from home. He did

12

not understand children at all, and was always grumbling at the noise they made, and the money they cost. Still, I think he was rather proud of Pip, and sometimes, if Nellie were prettily dressed, he would take her out with him in his dogcart.

He had offered to send the six of them to boarding school when he brought home his young girl-wife, but she would not hear of it.

At first they had tried living in the barracks, but after a time every one in the officers' quarters rose in revolt at the pranks of those graceless children, so Captain Woolcot took a house some distance up the Parramatta River, and in considerable bitterness of spirit removed his family there.

They liked the change immensely; for there was a big wilderness of a garden, two or three paddocks, numberless sheds for hide-and-seek, and, best of all, the water. Their father kept three beautiful horses, one at the barracks and a hunter and a good hack at Misrule; so, to make up, the children—not that they cared in the slightest—went about in shabby, out-at-elbow clothes, and much-worn boots. They were taught—all but Pip, who went to the grammar school—by a very third-class daily governess, who lived in mortal fear of her ignorance being found out by her pupils. As a matter of fact, they had found her out long ago, as children will, but it suited them very well not to be pushed on and made to work, so they kept the fact religiously to themselves.

CHAPTER 2

Fowl for Dinner

"Oh, don't the days seem lank and long
When all goes right and nothing wrong;
And isn't your life extremely flat
With nothing whatever to grumble at?"

I HOPE YOU ARE NOT quite deafened yet, for
though I have got through the introductions, tea is
not nearly finished, so we must stay in the nursery
a little longer. All the time I have been talking Pip
has been grumbling at the lack of good things. The
table was not very tempting, certainly; the cloth
looked as if it had been flung on, the china was
much chipped and battered, the tea was very weak,
and there was nothing to eat but great thick slices of
bread and butter. Still, it was the usual tea, and
everyone seemed surprised at Pip's outburst.

"My father and Esther" (they all called their
young stepmother by her Christian name) "are
having roast fowl, three vegetables, and four kinds
of pudding," he said angrily; "it isn't fair!"

"But we had dinner at one o'clock, Pip, and yours
is saved as usual," said Meg, pouring out tea with
a lavish allowance of hot water and sugar.

"Boiled mutton and carrots and rice pudding!"

14

returned her brother witheringly. "Why shouldn't *we* have roast fowl and custard and things?"

"Yes, why shouldn't we?" echoed little greedy Bunty, his eyes lighting up.

"What a lot it would take for all of us!" said Meg, cheerfully attacking the bread loaf.

"We're only children—let us be thankful for this nice thick bread and this abundance of melting butter," said Judy, in a good little tone.

Pip pushed his chair back from the table.

"I'm going down to ask for some roast fowl," he said, with a look of determination in his eyes. "I can't forget the smell of it, and they'd got a lot on the table—I peeped in the door."

He took up his plate and proceeded downstairs, returning presently, to the surprise of everyone, with quite a large portion on his plate.

"He couldn't very well refuse," he chuckled. "Colonel Bryant is there; but he looked a bit mad —here, Fizz, I'll go you halves."

Judy pushed up her plate eagerly at this unusually magnanimous offer, and received a very small division, a fifth part, perhaps, with great gratitude.

"I just *love* fowl," said Nell longingly; "I've a great mind to go down and ask for a wing—I believe he'd give it to me."

These disrespectful children, as I am afraid you will have noticed, always alluded to their father as "he."

Nell took up another plate, and departed slowly to the lower regions. She followed into the dining-room at the heels of the housemaid, and stood by the side of her father, her plate well behind her.

"Well, my little maid, won't you shake hands with me? What is your name?" said Colonel Bryant, tapping her cheek playfully.

Nell looked up with shy, lovely eyes.

"Elinor Woolcot, but they call me Nell," she said, holding out her left hand, since her right was occupied with the plate.

"What a little barbarian you are, Nell!" laughed her father; but he gave her a quick, annoyed glance. "Where is your right hand?"

She drew it slowly from behind and held out the cracked old plate. "I thought perhaps you would give me some fowl too," she said—"just a leg or a wing, or a bit of breast would do."

The Captain's brow darkened. "What is the meaning of this? Pip has just been to me, too. Have you nothing to eat in the nursery?"

"Only bread and butter, very thick," sighed Nellie.

Esther suppressed a smile with difficulty.

"But you had dinner, all of you, at one o'clock."

"Boiled mutton and carrots and rice pudding," said Nell mournfully.

Captain Woolcot severed a leg almost savagely and put it on her plate.

"Now run away; I don't know what has possessed you two to-night."

Nellie reached the door, then turned back.

"Oh, if you would just give me a wing for poor Meg—Judy had some of Pip's, but Meg hasn't any," she said, with a beautiful look of distress that quite touched Colonel Bryant.

16

Her father bit his lip, hacked off a wing in ominous silence, and put it upon her plate.

"Now run away, and don't let me have any more of this nonsense—dear." The last word was a terrible effort.

Nell's appearance with the two portions of fowl was hailed with uproarious applause in the nursery; Meg was delighted with her share, cut a piece off for Baby, and the meal went on merrily.

"Where's Bunty?" said Nell, pausing suddenly with a very clean drumstick in her fingers, "because I *hope* he hasn't gone too; someway I don't think Father was very pleased, especially as that man was there."

But that small youth had done so, and returned presently crestfallen.

"He wouldn't give me any—he told me to go away, and the man laughed, and Esther said we were very naughty—I got some feathered potatoes, though, from the table outside the door."

He opened his dirty little hands and dropped the uninviting feathered delicacy out upon the cloth.

"Bunty, you're a pig," sighed Meg, looking up from her book. She always read at the table, and this particular story was about some very refined, elegant girls.

"Pig yourself—all of you've had fowl but me, you greedy things!" retorted Bunty fiercely, and eating up his potato very fast.

"No, the General hasn't," said Judy and the old mischief light sprang up suddenly into her dark eyes.

" Now, Judy! " said Meg warningly; she knew too well what that particular sparkle meant.

" Oh, I'm not going to hurt you, you dear old thing," said Miss Judy, dancing down the room and bestowing a pat on her sister's fair head as she passed. " It's only the General, who's after havin' a bit o' fun."

She lifted him up out of the high chair, where he had been sitting drumming on the table with a spoon and eating sugar in the intervals.

" It's real action you're going for to see, General," she said, dancing to the door with him.

" Oh, Judy, what *are* you going to do? " said Meg entreatingly.

" Ju-Ju! " crowed the General, leaping almost out of Judy's arms, and scenting fun with the instinct of a veteran.

Down the passage they went, the other five behind to watch proceedings. Judy sat down with him on the last step.

" Boy want chuck-chuck, pretty chuck-chuck? " she said insidiously.

" Chuck-chuck, chuck-a-chuck," he gurgled, looking all around for his favourite friends.

" Dad got lots—all *this* many," said Judy, opening her arms very wide to denote the number in her father's possession. " Boydie go get them! "

" Chuck-chuck," crowed the General delightedly, and struggling to his feet—" find chuck-chuck."

" In there," whispered Judy, giving him a gentle push into the half-open dining-room door; " ask Dad."

18

Right across the room the baby tottered on his fat, unsteady little legs.

"Are the children *all* possessed to-night, Esther?" said the Captain, as his youngest son clutched wildly at his leg and tried to climb up it.

He looked down into the little dirty, dimpling face. "Well, General, and to what do we owe the honour of *your* presence?"

"Chuck-chuck, chuck-a-chuck, chuck, chuck, chuck," said the General, going down promptly upon all fours to seek for the feathered darlings Judy had said were here.

But Esther gathered up the dear, dirty-faced young rascal and bore him struggling out of the room. At the foot of the stairs she nearly stumbled over the rest of the family.

"Oh, you scamps, you bad, wicked imps!" she said, reaching out to box all their ears, and of course failing.

She sat down on the bottom stair to laugh for a second, then she handed the General to Pip.

"To-morrow," she said, standing up and hastily smoothing the rich hair that the General's hands had clutched gleefully—"to-morrow I shall beat every one of you with the broomstick."

They watched the train of her yellow silk dress disappear into the dining-room again, and returned slowly to the nursery and their interrupted tea.

CHAPTER 3

Virtue Not Always Rewarded

IT WAS NOT TO BE EXPECTED that such an occurrence could be passed entirely over, but then again it is difficult to punish seven children at the same time. At first Captain Woolcot had requested Esther to ask Miss Marsh, the governess, to give them all ten French verbs to learn; but, as Judy pointed out, the General and Baby and Bunty and Nell had not arrived at the dignity of French verbs yet, so such a punishment would be iniquitous. The sentence therefore had not been quite decided upon as yet, and everyone felt in an uncomfortable state of suspense.

"Your father says you're a disgraceful tribe," said the young stepmother slowly, sitting down on the nursery rocking-chair a day later. She had on a trailing morning wrapper of white muslin with cherry ribbons, but there was a pin doing duty for a button in one or two places and the lace was hanging off a bit at the sleeve.

"Meg, dear, you're very untidy, you know, and Judy's absolutely hopeless."

Meg was attired in an unbecoming green cashmere, with the elbows out and the plush torn off in several places, while Judy's exceedingly scant and faded pink zephyr had rents in several places, and the colour was hardly to be seen for fruit stains.

Meg coloured a little. "I know, Esther, and I'd like to be nicely dressed as well as anyone, but it really isn't worth mending these old things."

She picked up her book about the elegant girls who were disturbing her serenity and went over to the armchair with it.

"Well, Judy, you go and sew up those rents, and put some buttons on your frock." Esther spoke with unusual determination.

Judy's eyes snapped and sparkled.

"'Is that a dagger that I see before me, the handle to my hand? Come, let me grasp it,'" she said saucily, snatching one of the pins from Esther's dress, fastening her own with it, and dropping a curtsey.

Esther reddened a little now.

"That's the General, Judy: he always pulls the buttons off my wrappers when I play with him. But I'm forgetting. Children, I have bad news for you."

There was a breathless silence. Everyone crowded round her knees.

"Sentence has been proclaimed," said Judy dramatically: "let us shave our heads and don sackcloth."

"Your father says he cannot allow such conduct to go unpunished, especially as you have all been unusually tiresome lately; therefore you are all——"

"To be taken away and hanged by the neck until we are dead!"

"Be quiet, Judy. I have tried my best to beg

21

you off, but it only makes him more vexed. He says you are the untidiest, most unruly lot of children in Sydney, and he will punish you each time you do anything, and——"

"There shall be weeping and gnashing of teeth."

"Oh, shut up, Judy! Can't you let us hear?"

Pip put his hand over her mouth and held her by the hair while Esther told the news.

"None of you are to go to the pantomime. The seats were taken for Thursday night, and now, you very foolish children, you will all have to stay at home."

There was a perfect howl of dismay for a minute or two. They had all been looking forward to this treat for nearly a month, and the disappointment was a really bitter one to them all.

"Oh, I say, Esther, that's too bad, really! All the fellows at school have been." Pip's handsome face flushed angrily. "And for such a little thing, too!"

"Just because you had roast fowl for dinner," said Judy, in a half-choked voice. "Oh, Esther, why *couldn't* you have had cow, or horse, or hippopotamus—anything but roast fowl?"

"Couldn't you get round him, Esther?" Meg looked anxiously at her.

"Dear Esther, do!"

"Oh, you sweet, beautiful Essie, do try!"

They clung round her eagerly. Baby flung her arms round her neck and nearly choked her; Nell stroked her cheek; Pip patted her back, and besought her to "be a good fellow"; Bunty buried his

22

nose in her back hair and wept a silent tear; Meg clasped her hand in an access of unhappiness; the General gave a series of delighted squeaks; and Judy in her wretchedness smacked him for his pains.

Esther would do her best, beg as she had never done before, coax, beseech, wheedle, threaten; and they let her go at last with that assurance.

"Only I'd advise you all to be preternaturally good and quiet all day," she said, looking back from the doorway. "That would have most effect with him, and he is going to be at home all day."

Good! It was absolutely painful to witness the virtue of those children for the rest of the day.

It was holiday-time, and Miss Marsh was away, but not once did the sound of quarrelling, or laughing, or crying fly down to the lower regions.

"'Citizens of Rome, the eyes of the world are upon you!'" Judy had said solemnly, and all had promised so to conduct themselves that their father's heart could not fail to be melted.

Pip put on his school jacket, brushed his hair, took a pile of school books, and proceeded to the study where his father was writing letters, and where he was allowed to do his home-lessons.

"Well, what do you want?" said the Captain, with a frown. "No, it's no good coming to me about that pup, sir—I won't have you keep it."

"I came to study, sir," said Pip mildly. "I feel I'm a bit backward with my mathematics, so I won't waste all the holidays, when I'm costing you so much in school fees."

The Captain gave a little gasp and looked hard

at Pip; but the boy's face was so unsmiling and earnest that he was disarmed, and actually congratulated himself that his eldest son was at last seeing the error of his ways.

"There are those sets of problems in that drawer that I did when I was at school," he said graciously. "If they are of any use to you, you can get them out."

"Thanks awfully—they will be a great help," said Pip gratefully.

He examined them with admiration plainly depicted upon his face.

"How very clearly and correctly you worked, Father," he said with a sigh. "I wonder if ever I'll get as good as this! How old were you, Father, when you did them?"

"About your age," said the Captain, picking up the papers.

He examined them with his head on one side. He was rather proud of them, seeing he had utterly forgotten now how to work decimal fractions, and could not have done a quadratic equation to save his life.

"Still, I don't think you need be quite discouraged, Pip. I was rather beyond the other boys in my class in these subjects, I remember. We can't all excel in the same thing, and I'm glad to see you are beginning to realize the importance of work."

"Yes, Father."

Meg had betaken herself to the drawing-room, and was sitting on the floor before the music canterbury with scissors, thimble, and a roll of narrow blue ribbon on her knee, and all her father's songs, that he so often complained were falling to pieces, spread out before her.

He saw her once as he passed the door, and looked surprised and pleased.

"Thank you, Margaret: they wanted it badly. I am glad you can make yourself useful, after all," he said.

"Yes, Father."

Meg stitched on industriously.

He went back to his study, where Pip's head was at a studious, absorbed angle, and pyramids of books and sheaves of paper were on the table. He wrote two more letters, and there came a little knock at the door.

"Come in," he called; and there entered Nell.

She was carrying very carefully a little tray covered with a snow-white doyley, and on it were a glass of milk and a plate of mulberries. She placed it before him.

"I thought perhaps you would like a little lunch, Father," she said gently; and Pip was seized with a sudden coughing fit.

"My *dear* child!" he said.

He looked at it very thoughtfully.

"The last glass of milk I had, Nellie, was when I ·was Pip's age, and was Barlow's fag at Rugby. It made me ill, and I have never touched it since."

"But this won't hurt you. You will drink this?"

She gave him one of her most beautiful looks.

"I would as soon drink the water the maids wash up in, my child." He took a mulberry, ate it, and made a wry face. "They're not fit to eat."

"After you've eaten about six you don't notice

they're sour," she said eagerly. But he pushed them away.

"I'll take your word for it." Then he looked at her curiously. "What made you think of bringing me anything, Nellie? I don't ever remember you doing so before."

"I thought you might be hungry writing here so long," she said gently; and Pip choked again badly, and she withdrew.

Outside in the blazing sunshine Judy was mowing the lawn.

They only kept one man, and, as his time was so taken up with the horses and stable work generally, the garden was allowed to fall into neglect. More than once the Captain had spoken vexedly of the untidy lawns, and said he was ashamed for visitors to come to the house.

So Judy, brimming over with zeal, armed herself with an abnormally large scythe, and set to work on the long, long grass.

"Good heavens, Helen! you'll cut your legs off!" called her father, in an agitated tone.

He had stepped out on to the front veranda for a mild cigar after the mulberry just as she brought her scythe round with an admirable sweep and decapitated a whole army of yellow-helmeted dandelions.

She turned and gave him a beautiful smile.

"Oh, no, Father!—why, I'm quite a dab at mowing."

She gave it another alarming but truly scientific sweep.

"See that—and th-a-at—and tha-a-a-at!"

26

"Th-a-at" carried off a fragment of her dress, and "tha-a-a-at" switched off the top of a rose-bush; but there are details to everything, of course.

"Accidents *will* happen, even to the best regulated grass-cutters," she said composedly, and raising the scythe for a fresh circle.

"Stop immediately, Helen! Why ever can't you go and play quietly with your doll, and not do things like this?" said her father irascibly.

"An' I was afther doin' it just to pleasure him," she said, apparently addressing the dandelions.

"Well, it won't 'pleasure him' to have to provide you with cork legs and re-stock the garden," he said dryly. "Put it down."

"Sure, an' it's illigence itsilf this side: you wouldn't be afther leaving half undone, like a man with only one cheek shaved."

Judy affected an Irish brogue at intervals, for some occult reason of her own.

"Sure an' if ye'd jist stip down and examine it yirself, it's quite aisy ye'd be in yer moind."

The Captain hid a slight smile in his moustache. The little girl looked so comical, standing there in her short old pink frock, a broken-brimmed hat on her tangle of dark curls, her eyes sparkling, her face flushed, the great scythe in her hands, and the saucy words on her lips.

He came down and examined it: it was done excellently well, like most of the things Miss Judy attempted—mischief always included: and her little black-stockinged legs were still in a good state of preservation.

"Hum! Well, you can finish it then, as Pat's

busy. How did you learn to mow, young lady of wonderful accomplishments?" (he looked at her questioningly); "and what made you set yourself such a task?"

Judy gave her curls a quick push off her hot forehead.

"(*A*) Faix, it was inborn in me," she answered instantly; "and (*B*)—sure, and don't I lo-o-ove you and delaight to plaize you?"

He went in again slowly, thoughtfully. Judy always mystified him. He understood her the least of any of his children, and sometimes the thought of her worried him. At present she was only a sharp, clever, and frequently impertinent child; but he felt she was utterly different from the other six, and it gave him an aggrieved kind of feeling when he thought about it, which was not very often.

He remembered her own mother had often said she trembled for Judy's future. That restless fire of hers that shone out of her dancing eyes, and glowed scarlet on her cheeks in excitement, and lent amazing energy and activity to her young, lithe body, would either make a noble, daring, brilliant woman of her, or else she would be shipwrecked on rocks the others would never come to, and it would flame up higher and higher and consume her.

"Be careful of Judy" had been almost the last words of the anxious mother when, in the light that comes when the world's is going out, she had seen with terrible clearness the stones and briars in the way of that particular pair of small, eager feet.

28

And she had died, and Judy was stumbling right amongst them now, and her father could not "be careful" of her because he absolutely did not know how.

As he went up the veranda steps again and through the hall, he was wishing almost prayerfully she had not been cast in so different a mould from the others, wishing he could stamp out that strange flame in her that made him so uneasy at times. He gave a great puff at his cigar, and sighed profoundly; then he turned on his heel and went off toward the stables to forget it all.

The man was away, exercising one of the horses in the long paddock; but there was something stirring in the harness-room, so he went in.

There was a little, dripping wet figure standing over a great bucket, and dipping something in and out with charming vigour.

At the sound of his footsteps, Baby turned round and lifted a perspiring little face to his.

"I'se washing the kitsies for you, and Flibberty-Gibbet," she said beamingly.

He took a horrified step forward.

There were two favourite kittens of his, shivering, miserable, up to their necks in a lather of soapy water; and Flibberty-Gibbet, the beautiful little fox-terrier he had just bought for his wife, chained to a post, also wet, miserable, and woebegone, also undergoing the cleansing process, and being scrubbed and swilled till his very reason was tottering.

"They'se *so* clean and nicey—no horrid ole fleas 'n them now. *Aren't* you glad? You can let

29

Flibberty go on your bed now, and Kitsy Blackeye is——"

Poor Baby never finished her speech. She had a confused idea of hearing a little "swear-word" from her father, of being shaken in a most ungentle fashion and put outside the stable, while the unfortunate animals were dried and treated with great consideration.

But the worst was yet to come, and the results were so exceedingly bad that the young Woolcots determined never again to assume virtues that they had not.

Bunty, of course, desired to help the cause as strongly as the others, and to that end his first action was to go into his bedroom and perform startling ablutions with his face, neck, and hands. Then he took his soap-shiny countenance and red, much be-scrubbed hands downstairs, and sunned himself under his father's very nose, hoping to attract favourable comment.

But he was bidden irritably "go and play," and saw he would have to find fresh means of appeasement.

He wandered into the study, with vague thoughts of tidying the tidy bookshelves; but Dick was there, surrounded with books and whittling a stick for a catapult, so he went out again. Then he climbed the stairs and explored his father's bedroom and dressing-room. In the latter there was a wide field for his operations. A full-dress uniform was lying across a chair, and it struck Bunty the gold buttons were looking less bright than they should, so he spent a harmless quarter of an hour in polishing them up. Next, he burnished some spurs, which also was harmless. Then he cast about for fresh employment.

There was quite a colony of dusty boots in one corner of the room, and there was a great bottle of black, treacly looking varnish on the mantelpiece. Bunty conceived the brilliant idea of cleaning the whole lot and standing them in a neat row to meet his father's delighted eyes. He found a handkerchief on the floor, of superfine cambric, though dirty, poured upon it a liberal allowance of varnish, and attacked the first pair.

A bright polish rewarded him, for they were patent leather ones; but the next and the next and the next would not shine, however hard he rubbed. There was a step on the stair, the firm, well-known step of his father, and he paused a moment with a look of conscious virtue on his small shiny face.

But it fled all at once, and a look of horror replaced it. He had stuck the bottle on a great armchair for convenience, as he was sitting on the floor, and now he noticed it had fallen on its side and a black, horrid stream was issuing from its neck.

And it was the chair with the uniform on, and one of the sleeves was soaked with the stuff, and the beautiful white shirt that lay there, too, waiting for a button, was sticky, horrible! Bunty gave a wild, terrified look round the room for some place to efface himself, but there were no sheltering corners or curtains, and there was not time to get into the bedroom and under the bed. Near the window was a large-sized medicine chest, and in despair Bunty crushed himself into it, his legs huddled up, his head between his knees, and an ominous rattle of displaced bottles in his ears. The next minute his father was in the room.

"Great heavens! God bless my soul!" he said, and Bunty shivered from head to foot.

Then he said a lot of things very quickly—"foreign language," as Judy called it; kicked something over, and shouted "Esther!" in a terrifying tone. But Esther was down in one of the paddocks with the General, so there was no reply.

More foreign language, more stamping about.

Bunty's teeth chattered noisily; he put up his hand to hold his mouth together, and the cupboard, overbalanced, fell right over, precipitating its occupant right at his father's feet, and the bottles everywhere.

"I didn't—I haven't—'twasn't me—'twasn't my fault!" he howled, backing towards the door. "Hoo—yah—boo—hoo—ooo! Esther—boo—yah—Judy—oh—oh—h! oh—oh—h—h—h—h!" As might be expected, his father had picked up a strap that lay conveniently near, and was giving his son a very fair taste of it.

"Oh—h—h—h! o—o—h! o—o—h! ah—h—h! 'twasn't me—'twasn't my fault—it's Pip and Judy—oh—h—h—h! hoo—the pant'mime! boo—hoo! ah—h—h—h—you're killing me! hoo—boo! I was only d—doin' it—oh—hoo—ah—h—h! d—doin' it to p—please—boo—oo—oo! to p—please you!"

His father paused with uplifted strap. "And that's why all the others are behaving in so strange a fashion? Just for me to take them to the panto-mime?"

Bunty wriggled himself free. " Boo—hoo—yes! but not me—I didn't—I never—true's faith— oh—h—h—hoo—yah! it wasn't my fault, it's all the others—boo—hoo—hoo! hit them the rest."

He got three more smart cuts, and then fled howling and yelling to the nursery, where he fell on the floor and kicked and rolled about as if he were half killed.

" You sn—n—n—n—neaks! " he sobbed, addressing the others, who had flown from all parts at his noisy outcry, " you m—m——mean p—p—p—pigs! I h—hadn't n—n—no fo—o—ow-l, and I've h—h—had all the b—b—b—beating! y—you s—s—sn—n—neaks! oh—h—h—h! ah—h—h—h! oh—h—h—h! oh—h—h—h! I'm b—b—bleedin' all over, I kno—o—o—ow! "

They couldn't help laughing a bit; Bunty was always so irresistibly comic when he was hurt ever so little; but still they comforted him as well as they could, and tried to find out what had happened.

Esther came in presently, looking very worried.

" Well? " they said in a breath.

" You really are the most exasperating children," she said vexedly.

" But the pantomime—quick, Esther—have you asked him? " they cried impatiently.

" The pantomime! He says he would rather make it worth Mr. Rignold's while to take it off the boards than that one of you should catch a glimpse of it—and it serves you very well right! Meg, for goodness' sake give Baby some dry clothes—just look at her; and, Judy, if you have any feeling for me, take off that frock. Bunty, you wicked boy, I'll

c   33 call your father if you don't stop that noise. Nell, take the scissors from the General, he'll poke his eyes out, bless him."

The young stepmother leaned back in her chair and looked round her tragically. She had never seen her husband so thoroughly angered, and her beautiful lips quivered when she remembered how he had seemed to blame her for it all.

Meg hadn't moved; the water was trickling slowly off Baby's clothes and making a pool on the floor, Bunty was still giving vent to spasmodic boos and hoos, Judy was whistling stormily, and the General, mulcted of the scissors, was licking his own muddy shoe all over with his dear little red tongue.

A sob rose in her throat, two tears welled up in her eyes and fell down her smooth, lovely cheeks.

"Seven of you, and I'm only twenty!" she said pitifully. "Oh! it's too bad—oh dear! it *is* too bad."

CHAPTER 4

The General Sees Active Service

*"My brain it teems
With endless schemes,
Both good and new."*

IT WAS A DAY AFTER "the events narrated in the last chapter," as story-book parlance has it. And Judy, with a wrathful look in her eyes, was sitting on the nursery table, her knees touching her chin and her thin brown hands clasped round them.

"It's a shame," she said, "it's a burning, wicked shame! What's the use of fathers in the world, I'd like to know!"

"Oh, Judy!" said Meg, who was curled up in an armchair, deep in a book. But she said it mechanically, and only as a matter of duty, being three years older than Judy.

"Think of the times we could have if he didn't live with us," Judy continued, calmly disregardful. "Why, we'd have fowl three times a day, and the pantomime seven nights a week."

Nell suggested that it was not quite usual to have pantomimic performances on the seventh day, but Judy was not daunted.

"I'd have a kind of church pantomime," she said

35

thoughtfully—"beautiful pictures and things about the Holy Land, and the loveliest music, and beautiful children in white, singing hymns, and bright colours all about, and no collection plates to take your only threepenny bit—oh! and no sermons or litanies, of course."

"Oh, Judy!" murmured Meg, turning a leaf.

Judy unclasped her hands, and then clasped them again more tightly than before. "Six whole tickets wasted—thirty beautiful shillings—just because we have a father!"

"He sent them to the Digby-Smiths," Bunty volunteered, "and wrote on the envelope, '*With compts.*—J. C. Woolcot.'"

Judy moaned. "Six horrid little Digby-Smiths sitting in the theatre watching our fun with their six horrid little eyes," she said bitterly.

Bunty, who was mathematically inclined, wanted to know why they wouldn't look at it through their twelve horrid little eyes, and Judy laughed and came down from the table, after expressing a wicked wish that the little Digby-Smiths might all tumble over the dress-circle rail before the curtain rose. Meg shut her book with a hurried bang.

"Has Pip gone yet? Father'll be awfully cross. Oh *dear*, what a head I've got!" she said. "Where's Esther? Has anyone seen Esther?"

"My *dear* Meg!" Judy said; "why, it's at least two hours since Esther went up the drive before your very nose. She's gone to Waverly—why, she came in and told you, and said she trusted you to see about the coat, and you said, ''M—'m! all right.'"

Meg gave a startled look of recollection. "Did I have to clean it?" she asked in a frightened tone, and pushing her fair hair back from her forehead. "Oh, girls! what *was* it I had to do?"

"Clean with benzine, iron while wet, put in a cool place to keep warm, and bake till brown," said Judy promptly. "*Surely* you heard, Margaret? Esther was at such pains to explain."

Meg ruffled her hair again despairingly. "What shall I do?" she said, actual tears springing to her eyes. "What will Father say? Oh, Judy, you might have reminded me."

Nell slipped an arm round her neck. "She's only teasing, Megsie; Esther did it and left it ready in the hall—you've only to give it to Pip. Pat has to take the dogcart into town this afternoon to have the back seat mended, and Pip's going in it, too, that's all, and they're putting the horse in now; you're not late."

It was the coat Bunty had done his best to spoil that all the trouble was about. It belonged, as I said, to the Captain's full-dress uniform, and was wanted for a dinner at the Barracks this same evening. And Esther had been sponging and cleaning at it all the morning, and had left directions that it was to be taken to the Barracks in the afternoon.

Presently the dogcart came spinning round to the door in great style, Pip driving and Pat looking sulkily on. They took the coat parcel and put it carefully under the seat, and were preparing to start again, when Judy came out upon the veranda, holding the General in an uncomfortable position in her arms.

"You come, too, Fizz, there's heaps of room—there's no reason you shouldn't," Pip said suddenly.

"Oh—h—h!" said Judy, her eyes sparkling. She took a rapid step forward and lifted her foot to get in.

"Oh, I say!" remonstrated Pip, "you'll have to put on something over that dress, old girl—it's all over jam and things."

Judy shot herself into the hall and returned with her ulster; she set the General on the floor for a minute while she donned it, then picked him up and handed him up to Pip.

"He'll have to come, too," she said; "I promised Esther I wouldn't let him out of my sight for a minute; she's getting quite nervous about him lately —thinks he'll get broken."

Pip grumbled a minute or two, but the General gave a gurgling, captivating laugh and held up his arms, so he took him up and held him while Judy clambered in.

"We can come back in the tram to the Quay, and then get a boat back," she said, squeezing the baby on the seat between them. "The General loves going on the water."

Away they sped; down the neglected carriage drive, out of the gates, and away down the road. Pip, Judy of the shining eyes, the General devouring his thumb, and Pat smiling-faced once more because in possession of the reins.

A wind from the river swept through the belt of gum trees on the Crown lands, and sent the young red blood leaping through their veins; it played havoc with Judy's curls, and dyed her brown cheeks

38

a warm red; it made the General kick and laugh and grow restive, and caused Pip to stick his hat on the back of his head and whistle joyously.

Until town was reached, when they were forced to yield somewhat to the claims of conventionality.

On the way to Paddington a gentleman on horseback slackened pace a little. Pip took off his hat with a flourish, and Judy gave a frank, pleased smile, for it was a certain old Colonel they had known for years, and had cause to remember his good-humour and liberality.

"Well, my little maid—well, Philip, lad," he said, smiling genially, while his horse danced round the dogcart—"and the General too—where are you all off to?"

"The Barracks—I'm taking something up for the governor," Pip answered. Judy was watching the plunging horse with admiring eyes. "And then we're going back home."

The old gentleman managed, in spite of the horse's tricks, to slip his hand in his pocket. "Here's something to make yourselves ill with on the way," he said, handing them two half-crowns; "but don't send me the doctor's bill."

He flicked the General's cheek with his whip, gave Judy a nod, and cantered off.

The children looked at each other with sparkling eyes.

"Coconuts," Pip said, "and tarts and toffee, and save the rest for a football?" Judy shook her head.

"Where do *I* come in?" she said. "You'd keep the football at school. I vote pink jujubes, and ice-creams, and a wax doll."

"A wax grandmother!" Pip retorted; "you wouldn't be such a girl, I hope." Then he added, with almost pious fervour, "Thank goodness you've always hated dolls, Fizz."

Judy gave a sudden leap in her seat, almost upsetting the General, and bringing down upon her head a storm of reproaches from the coachman. "*I* know!" she said; "and we're almost half-way there now. Oh—h—h! it *will* be lovely."

Pip urged her to explain herself.

"Bondi Aquarium—skating, boats, merry-go-round, switchback threepence a go!" she returned succinctly.

"Good iron," Pip whistled softly, while he revolved the thing in his mind. "There'd be something over, too, to get some tucker with, and perhaps something for the football, too." Then his brow clouded.

"There's the kid—whatever did you go bringing him for? Just like a girl, to spoil everything!"

Judy looked nonplussed. "I quite forgot him," she said, vexedly. "Couldn't we leave him somewhere? Couldn't we ask someone to take care of him while we go? Oh, it would be *too* bad to have to give it up just because of him. It's beginning to rain, too; we couldn't take him with us."

They were at the foot of Barrack Hill now, and Pat told them they must get out and walk the rest of the way up, or he would never get the dogcart finished to take back that evening.

Pip tumbled out and took the General, all in a bunched-up heap, and Judy alighted carefully after him, the precious coat parcel in her arms. And they

40

walked up the asphalt hill to the gate leading to the officers' quarters in utter silence.

"Well?" Pip said querulously, as they reached the top. "Be quick; haven't you thought of anything?"

That levelling of brows, and pursing of lips, always meant deep and intricate calculation on his sister's part, as he knew full well.

"Yes," Judy said quietly. "I've got a plan that will do, I think." Then a sudden fire entered her manner.

"Who is the General's father? Tell me that," she said, in a rapid, eager way; "and isn't it right and proper fathers should look after their sons? And doesn't he deserve we should get even with him for doing us out of the pantomime? And isn't the Aquarium too lovely to miss?"

"Well?" Pip said; his slower brain did not follow such rapid reasoning.

"Only I'm going to leave the General here at the Barracks for a couple of hours till we come back, his father being the proper person to watch over him." Judy grasped the General's small fat hand in a determined way, and opened the gate.

"Oh, I say," remarked Pip, "we'll get in an awful row, you know, Fizz. I don't think we'd better—I don't really, old girl."

"Not a bit," said Judy stoutly—"at least, only a bit, and the Aquarium's worth that. Look how it's raining; the child will get croup, or rheumatism, or something if we take him; there's Father standing over on the green near the tennis-court talking to a man. I'll slip quietly along the veranda and into

41

his own room, and put the coat and the General on the bed; then I'll tell a soldier to go and tell Father his parcels have come, and while he's gone I'll fly back to you, and we'll catch the tram and go to the Aquarium."

Pip whistled again, softly. He was used to bold proposals from this sister of his, but this was beyond everything. "B—b—but," he said uneasily, "but, Judy, whatever would he do with that kid for two mortal hours?"

"Mind him," Judy returned promptly. "It's a pretty thing if a father can't mind his own child for two hours. Afterwards, you see, when we've been to the Aquarium, we will come back and fetch him, and we can explain to Father how it was raining, and that we thought we'd better not take him with us for fear of rheumatism, and that we were in a hurry to catch the tram, and as he wasn't in his room we just put him on the bed till he came. Why, Pip, it's beautifully simple!"

Pip still looked uncomfortable. "I don't like it, Fizz," he said again; "he'll be in a fearful wax."

Judy gave him one exasperated look. "Go and see if that's the Bondi tram coming," she said; and, glad of a moment's respite, he went down the path again to the pavement and looked down the hill. When he turned round again she had gone.

He stuck his hands in his pockets and walked up and down the path a few times. "Fizz'll get us hanged yet," he muttered, looking darkly at the door in the wall through which she had disappeared.

He pushed his hat to the back of his head and

stared gloomily at his boots, wondering what would be the consequences of this new mischief. There was a light footfall beside him.

"Come on," said Judy, pulling his sleeve; "it's done now, come on, let's go and have our fun; have you got the money safe?"

It was two o'clock as they passed out of the gate and turned their faces up the hill to the tram stopping-place. And it was half-past four when they jumped out of a town-bound tram and entered the gates again to pick up their charge.

Such an afternoon as they had had! Once inside the Aquarium, even Pip had put his conscience qualms on one side, and bent all his energies to enjoying himself thoroughly. And Judy was like a little mad thing. She spent a shilling of her money on the switchback railway, pronouncing the swift, bewildering motion "heavenly." The first journey made Pip feel sick, so he eschewed a repetition of it, and watched Judy go off from time to time, waving gaily from the perilous little car, almost with his heart in his mouth. Then they hired a pair of roller skates each, and bruised themselves black and blue with heavy falls on the asphalt. After that they had a ride on the merry-go-round, but Judy found it tame after the switchback, and refused to squander a second threepence upon it, contenting herself with watching Pip fly round, and madly running by his side to keep up as long as she could. They finished the afternoon with a prolonged inspection of the fish-tanks, a light repast of jam tarts of questionable freshness, and twopennyworth of peanuts. And, as I said, it was half-past four as they

43

hastened up the path again to the top gate of the Barracks.

"I *hope* he's been good," Judy said, as she turned the handle. "Yes, you come, too, Pip"—for that young gentleman hung back one agonized second. "Twenty kicks or blows divided by two only make ten, you see."

They went up the long stone veranda and stopped at one door.

There was a little knot of young officers laughing and talking close by.

"Take my word, 'twas as good as a play to see Wooly grabbing his youngster, and stuffing it into a cab, and getting in himself, all with a look of ponderous injured dignity," one said, and laughed at the recollection.

Another blew away a cloud of cigar smoke. "It was a jolly little beggar," he said. "It doubled its fists and landed His High Mightiness one in the eye; and then its shoe dropped off, and we all rushed to pick it up, and it was muddy and generally dilapidated, and old Wooly went red slowly up to his ear-tips as he tried to put it on."

A little figure stepped into the middle of the group—a little figure with an impossibly short and shabby ulster, thin black-stockinged legs, and a big hat crushed over a tangle of curls.

"It is my father you are speaking of," she said, her head very high, her tone haughty, "and I cannot tell where your amusement is. Is my father here, or did I hear you say he had gone away?"

Two of the men looked foolish, the third took off his cap.

" I am sorry you should have overheard us, Miss Woolcot," he said pleasantly. "Still, there is no irreparable harm done, is there? Yes, your father has gone away in a cab. He couldn't imagine how the little boy came on his bed, and, as he couldn't keep him here very well, I suppose he has taken him home."

Something like a look of shame came into Judy's bright eyes.

" I am afraid I must have put my father to some inconvenience," she said quietly. "It was I who left the Gen—my brother here, because I didn't know what to do with him for an hour or two. But I quite meant to take him home myself. Has he been gone long?"

" About half an hour," the officer said, and tried not to look amused at the little girl's old-fashioned manner.

" Ah, thank you. Perhaps we can catch him up. Come on, Pip," and, nodding in a grave, distant manner, she turned away, and went down the veranda and through the gate with her brother.

" A nice hole we're in," he said.

Judy nodded.

" It's about the very awfullest thing we've ever done in our lives. Fancy the governor carting that child all the way from here! Oh, lor'! "

Judy nodded again.

" Can't you speak?" he said irritably. "You've got us into this—I didn't want to do it; but I'll stand by you, of course. Only you'll have to think of something quick."

45

Judy bit three finger-tips off her right-hand glove, and looked melancholy.

"There's absolutely nothing to do, Pip," she said slowly. "I didn't think it would turn out like this. I suppose we'd better just go straight back and hand ourselves over for punishment. He'll be too angry to hear any sort of an excuse, so we'd better just grin and bear whatever he does to us. I'm really sorry, too, that I made a laughing-stock of him up there."

Pip was explosive. He called her a little ass and a gowk and a stupid idiot for doing such a thing, and she did not reproach him or answer back once.

They caught a tram and went into Sydney, and afterwards to the boat. They ensconced themselves in a corner at the far end, and discussed the state of affairs with much seriousness. Then Pip got up and strolled about a little to relieve his feelings, coming back in a second with a white, scared face.

"He's on the boat," he said, in a horrified whisper.

"Where—where—where? what—what—what?" Judy cried, unintentionally mimicking a long-buried monarch.

"In the cabin, looking as glum as a boiled wallaby, and hanging on to the poor little General as if he thinks he'll fly away."

Judy looked a little frightened for the first time.

"Can't we hide? Don't let him see us. It wouldn't be any good offering to take the General now. We're in for it now, Pip—there'll be no quarter."

Pip groaned; then Judy stood up.

" Let's creep down as far as the engine," she said, "and see if he does look very bad."

They made their way cautiously along the deck, and took up a position where they could see without being seen. The dear little General was sitting on the seat next to his stern father, who had a firm hold of the back of his woolly pelisse. He was sucking his little dirty hand, and casting occasional longing glances at his tan shoe, which he knew was delicious to bite. Once or twice he had pulled it off and conveyed it to his mouth, but his father intercepted it, and angrily buttoned it on again in its rightful place. He wanted, too, to slither off the horrid seat, and crawl all over the deck, and explore the ground under the seats, and see where the puffing noise came from; but there was that iron grasp on his coat that no amount of wriggling would move. No wonder the poor child looked unhappy!

At last the boat stopped at a wharf not far from Misrule, and the Captain alighted, carrying his small dirty son gingerly in his arms. He walked slowly up the red road along which the dogcart had sped so blithesomely some six or seven hours ago, and Judy and Pip followed at a respectful—a very respectful—distance. At the gate he saw them, and gave a large, angry beckon for them to come up. Judy went very white, but obeyed instantly, and Pip, pulling himself together, brought up the rear.

Afterwards Judy only had a very indistinct remembrance of what happened during the next half-hour. She knew there was a stormy scene, in which Esther and the whole family came in for an immense amount of vituperation.

47

Then Pip received a thrashing, in spite of Judy's persistent avowal that it was all her fault, and Pip hadn't done anything. She remembered wondering whether she would be treated as summarily as Pip, so angry was her father's face as he pushed the boy aside and stood looking at her, riding whip in hand.

But he flung it down and laid a heavy hand on her shrinking shoulder.

"Next Monday," he said slowly—"next Monday morning you will go to boarding school. Esther, kindly see Helen's clothes are ready for boarding school—next Monday morning."

CHAPTER 5

"Next Monday Morning"

THERE WAS A TRUNK standing in the hall, and a large, much-travelled portmanteau, and there were labels on them that said: "Miss Helen Woolcot, The Misses Burton, Mount Victoria."

In the nursery breakfast was proceeding spasmodically. Meg's blue eyes were all red and swollen with crying, and she was still sniffing audibly as she poured out the coffee. Pip had his hands in his pockets and stood on the hearthrug, looking gloomily at a certain plate, and refusing breakfast altogether; the General was crashing his own mug and plate joyously together; and Bunty was eating bread and butter in stolid silence.

Judy, white-faced and dry-eyed, was sitting at the table, and Nell and Baby were clinging to either arm. All the three days between that black Thursday and this doleful morning she had been obstinately uncaring. Her spirits had never seemed higher, her eyes brighter, her tongue sharper, than during that interval of days; and she had pretended to everyone, and her father, that she especially thought boarding school must be great fun, and that she should enjoy it immensely.

But this morning she had collapsed altogether.

D

49

All the time before, her hot, childish heart had been telling her that her father could not really be so cruel, that he did not really mean to send her away among strangers, away from dear, muddled old Misrule and all her sisters and brothers; he was only saying it to frighten her, she kept saying to herself, and she would show him she was not a chicken-hearted baby.

But on Sunday night, when she saw a trunk carried downstairs and filled with her things and labelled with her name, a cold hand seemed to close about her heart. Still, she said to herself, he was doing all this to make it seem more real.

But now it was morning, and she could disbelieve it no longer. Esther had come to her bedside and kissed her sorrowfully, her beautiful face troubled and tender. She had begged as she had never done before for a remission of poor Judy's sentence, but the Captain was adamant. It was she and she only who was always ringleader in everything; the others would behave when she was not there to incite them to mischief and go she should. Besides, he said, it would be the making of her. It was an excellent school he had chosen for her; the ladies who kept it were kind, but very firm, and Judy was being ruined for want of a firm hand. Which, indeed, was in a measure true.

Judy sat bolt upright in bed at the sight of Esther's sorrowful face.

"It's no good, dear; there's no way out of it," she said gently. "But you'll go like a brave girl, won't you, Ju-Ju? You always were the sort to die game, as Pip says."

Judy gulped down a great lump in her throat, and her poor little face grew white and drawn.

"It's all right, Essie. There, you go on down to breakfast," she said, in a voice that only shook a little; "and please leave me the General, Esther; I'll bring him down with me."

Esther deposited her little fat son on the pillow, and with one loving backward glance went out of the door.

And Judy pulled the little lad down into her arms, and covered the bedclothes right over both their heads, and held him in a fierce, almost desperate clasp for a minute or two, and buried her face in his soft, dimpled neck, and kissed it till her lips ached.

He fought manfully against these troublesome proceedings, and at last objected, with an angry scream, to being suffocated. So she flung back the clothes and got out of bed, leaving him to burrow about among the pillows, and pull feathers out of a hole in one of them.

She dressed in a quick nervous fashion, did her hair with more care than usual, and then picked up the General and took him along the passage into the nursery. All the others were here, and, with Esther, were evidently discussing her. The three girls looked tearful and protesting; Pip had just been brought to book for speaking disrespectfully of his father, and was looking sullen; and Bunty, not knowing what else to do at such a crisis, had fallen to catching flies, and was viciously taking off their wings.

It was a wretched meal. The bell sounded for

the downstairs breakfast, and Esther had to go. Everyone offered Judy everything on the table, and spoke gently and politely to her. She seemed to be apart from them, a person not to be lightly treated in the dignity of this great trouble. Her dress, too, was quite new—a neat blue serge fresh from the dressmaker's hands; her boots were blacked and bright, her stockings guiltless of ventilatory chasms. All this helped to make her a Judy quite different from the harum-scarum one of a few days back, who used to come to breakfast looking as if her clothes had been pitchforked upon her.

Baby addressed herself to her porridge for one minute, but the next her feelings overcame her, and, with a little wail, she rushed round the table to Judy, and hung on her arm sobbing. This destroyed the balance of the whole company. Nell got the other arm and swayed to and fro in an access of misery. Meg's tears rained down into her teacup; Pip dug his heel in the hearthrug, and wondered what was the matter with his eyes; and even Bunty's appetite for bread and butter diminished.

Judy sat there silent; she had pushed back her unused plate, and sat regarding it with an expression of utter despair on her young face. She looked like a miniature tragedy queen going to immediate execution.

Presently Bunty got off his chair, covered up his coffee with his saucer to keep the flies out, and solemnly left the room. In a minute he returned with a pickle bottle, containing an enormous green frog.

"You can have it to keep for your very own,

Judy," he said, in a tone of almost reckless sadness. "It'll keep you amused, perhaps, at school."

Self-sacrifice could go no further, for this frog was the darling of Bunty's heart.

This stimulated the others; everyone fetched some offering to lay at Judy's shrine for a keepsake. Meg brought a bracelet, plaited out of the hair of a defunct pet pony. Pip gave his three-bladed pocket-knife, Nell a pot of musk that she had watered and cherished for a year, Baby had a broken-nosed doll that was the Benjamin of her large family.

"Put them in the trunk, Meg—there's room on top, I think," Judy said in a choking voice, and deeply touched by these gifts. "Oh! and, Bunty, dear! put a cork over the f—f—frog, will you? it might get lost, poor thing! in that b—b—big box."

"All right," said Bunty. "You'll take c—c—care of it, w—won't you, Judy? Oh dear, oh—h—h! — boo—hoo!"

Then Esther came in, still troubled-looking.

"The dogcart is round," she said. "Are you ready, Ju, dearest? Dear little Judy! be brave, little old woman."

But Judy was white as death, and utterly limp. She suffered Esther to put her hat on, to help her into her new jacket, to put her gloves into her hand. She submitted to being kissed by the whole family, to be half carried downstairs by Esther, to be kissed again by the girls, then by the two good-natured domestics, who, in spite of her peccadilloes, had a warm place in their hearts for her.

Esther and Pip lifted her into the dogcart, and she sat in a little, huddled-up way, looking down at the group on the veranda with eyes that were absolutely tragic in their utter despair. Her father came out, buttoning his overcoat, and saw the look.

"What foolishness is this?" he said irascibly. "Esther—great heavens! are you making a goose of yourself, too?"—there were great tears glistening in his wife's beautiful eyes. "Upon my soul, one would think I was going to take the child to be hanged, or at least was going to leave her in a penitentiary."

A great dry sob broke from Judy's white lips.

"If you'll let me stay, Father, I'll never do another thing to vex you; and you can thrash me instead, ever so hard."

It was her last effort, her final hope, and she bit her poor quivering lip till it bled while she waited for his answer.

"Let her stay—oh! do let her stay, we'll be good always," came in a chorus from the veranda. And, "Let her stay, John, *please!*" Esther called, in a tone as entreating as any of the children.

But the Captain sprang into the dogcart and seized the reins from Pat in a burst of anger.

"I think you're all demented!" he cried. "She's going to a thoroughly good home, I've paid a quarter in advance already, and I can assure you good people I'm not going to waste it."

He gave the horse a smart touch with the whip, and in a minute the dogcart had flashed out of the gate, and the small, unhappy face was lost to sight.

CHAPTER 6

The Sweetness of Sweet Sixteen

———— ❧ ————

"She is not yet so old
But she may learn: happier than this,
She is not bred so dull but she can learn."

MEG'S HAIR HAD ALWAYS BEEN PRETTY,
but during the last two months she had cut herself
a fringe, and begun to torture it up in curl papers
every night. And in her private drawer she kept a
jam tin filled with oatmeal, that she used in the
water every time she washed, having read it was
a great complexion beautifier. And nightly she
rubbed vaseline on her hands and slept in old kid
gloves. And her spare money went in the purchase
of "Freckle Lotion," to remove that slight powdering of warm brown sun-kisses that somehow lent a
certain character to her face.

All these things were the outcome of being sixteen, and having found a friend of seventeen.

Aldith MacCarthy learnt French from the
same teacher that Meg was going to twice a
week, and after an exchange of chocolates, hair-
ribbons, and family confidences a friendship sprang
up.

Aldith had three grown-up sisters, whom she aped

55

in everything, and was considerably wiser in the world than simple-minded, romantic Meg.

She lent Meg novels, *Family Herald Supplements, Young Ladies' Journals*, and such publications, and the young girl took to them with avidity, surprised at the new world into which they took her; for Charlotte Yonge and Louisa Alcott and Miss Wetherall had hitherto formed her simple and wholesome fare.

Meg began to dream rose-coloured dreams of the time when her fair, shining hair should be gathered up into " a simple knot at the back of her head " or "brushed into a regal coronet," these being the styles in which the heroines in the novels invariably dressed their hair. A pigtail done in three was very unromantic. That was why, as a sort of compromise, she cut herself a fringe and began to frizz out the end of her plait. Her father stared at her, and said she looked like a shop-girl, when first he noticed it, and Esther told her she was a stupid child; but the looking-glass and Aldith reassured her.

The next thing was surreptitiously to lengthen her dresses, which were at the short-long stage. In the privacy of her own bedroom she took the skirts of two or three of her frocks off the band, inserted a piece of lining for lengthening purposes, and then added a frill to the waists of her bodices to hide the join. This dropped the skirts a good two inches, and made her look quite a tall, slim figure, as she was well aware.

And none of these things were very harmful.

But Aldith gradually grew dissatisfied with her waist.

"You're at least twenty-three, Marguerite," she said once, quite in a horrified way.

She never called her friend Meg, pronouncing that name to be "too domestic and altogether unlovely."

Meg glanced from her own waist to her friend's slender, beautiful one, and sighed profoundly.

"What ought I to be?" she said in a low tone; and Aldith had answered, "Eighteen—or nineteen, Marguerite, at the most; true symmetrical grace can never be obtained with a waist twenty-three inches round."

Aldith had not only made statements and comparisons, she had given her friend practical advice, and shown her how the thing was to be done. And every night and morning Meg pulled away ruthlessly at her corset laces, and crushed her beautiful little body into narrower space. She had already brought it within a girdle of twenty-one inches, which was a clear saving of two, and she had taken in all her dresses at the seams.

But she gave up the evening game of cricket, and she never made one at rounders now, much to the others' disgust. No one, to look at the sweet blossom-like face, and soft, calm eyes, could have guessed what torture was being felt beneath the now pretty, well-fitting dress body. To walk quickly was positive pain; to stoop, almost agony; but she endured it all with a heroism worthy of a truly noble cause.

"How long shall I have to go on like this, Aldith?" she asked once faintly, after a French lesson that she had scarcely been able to sit through.

And the older girl answered carelessly, " Oh, you mustn't leave it off, of course, but you don't feel it at all after a bit."

With which assurance Meg pursued her painful course.

Esther, the only person in a position to exercise any authority in the matter, had not noticed at all, and, indeed, had she done so would not have thought very gravely of it, for it was only four years since she, too, had been sixteen, and a " waist " had been the most desirable thing on earth.

Once she had said unwittingly:

" What a nice little figure you are getting, Meg; this new dressmaker certainly fits better than Miss Quinn"; and foolish Meg, with a throb of delight, had redoubled her efforts.

Lynx-eyed Judy would have found her out long ago, and laughed her to utter shame, but unfortunately for Meg's constitution she was still at school, it being now the third month of her absence.

Aldith only lived about twenty minutes' walk from Misrule, so the two girls were always together. Twice a week they went down to town in the river-boat to learn how to inquire, in polite French, " Has the baker's young daughter the yellow hat, brown gloves, and umbrella of the undertaker's niece? " And twice a week, after they had answered irrelevantly, " No, but the surgeon had some beer, some mustard, and the dinner-gong," Aldith conducted her friend slowly up and down that happy hunting-ground of Sydney youth and fashion—the Block. " Just see how many hats I'll get taken off," Miss Aldith would say as they started; and by the end of the time Meg would say longingly, "How *lovely* it must be to know crowds of gentlemen like you do."

Sometimes one or two of them would stop and exchange a word or two, and then Aldith would formally introduce Meg; often, however, the latter, who was sharp enough for all her foolishness, would fancy she detected a patronizing, amused air in these gentlemen's manners. As, indeed, there often was; they were chiefly men whom Aldith had met at dances and tennis in her own home, and who thought that young lady a precocious child who wanted keeping in the schoolroom a few more years.

One day Aldith came to Misrule brimming over with mysterious importance. "Come down the garden, Marguerite," she said, taking no notice whatever of Baby, who had, with much difficulty, beguiled her eldest sister into telling her the ever delightful legend of the three little pigs.

"Oh, no, by the hair of my chiny-chin-chin, then I'll huff and I'll puff and I'll blow your house in," had only been said twice, and the exciting part was still to come.

Baby looked up with stormy eyes.

"Go away, Aldiff," she said.

"Miss MacCarthy, Baby, dear," Meg suggested gently, catching Aldith's half-scornful smile.

"*Aldiff*," repeated Baby obstinately. Then she relented, and put one caressing little arm round her sister's neck.

"I will say Miff MacCarfy iss you will say ze uzzer little pig, too."

59

"Oh, send her away, Marguerite, do," Aldith said impatiently, "I have an enthralling secret to tell you, and I'll have to go soon."

Meg looked interested immediately.

"Run away, Baby, dear," she said, kissing the disappointed little face; "go and play Noah's Ark with Bunty, and I'll finish the piggies to-night or to-morrow."

"But I want them *now*," Baby said insistently.

Meg pushed her gently aside. "No, run away, pet —run away at once like a good girl, and I'll tell you Red Riding Hood, too, to-morrow."

Baby looked up at her sister's guest.

"You are a horrid old pig, Aldiff MacCarfy," she said, with slow emphasis, "an' I hates you hard, an' we all hates you here, 'cept Meg; and Pip says you're ze jammiest girl out, an' I wis' a drate big ziant would come and huff and puff and blow you into ze middlest part of ze sea."

Aldith laughed, a little aggravating grown-up laugh, that put the finishing touch to Baby's anger. She put out her little hand and gave the guest's arm in its muslin sleeve a sharp, scientific pinch that Pip had taught her. Then she fled madly away down the long paddocks, to the bit of bush beyond.

"Insufferable," Aldith muttered angrily, and it needed all Meg's apologies and coaxings to get her into an amiable frame of mind again, and to induce her to communicate the enthralling secret. At last, however, it was imparted, with great impressiveness. Aldith's eldest sister was engaged, engaged to be married! Oh! wasn't it heavenly? Wasn't it romantic?—and to the gentleman with the long fair moustache who had been so much at their house lately.

"I knew it would come—I have seen it coming for a long time. Oh, I'm not easily blinded," Aldith said. "I know true love when I see it. Though certainly for myself I should prefer a dark moustache, should not you, Marguerite?"

"Ye—es," said Meg. Her views were hardly formed yet on the subject.

"Jet black, with waxed ends, very stiff," Aldith continued thoughtfully, "and a soldierly carriage, and very long black lashes."

"So should I," Meg said, fired in a moment. "Like Guy Deloraine in *Angelina's Ambition*."

Aldith put her arm more tightly round her friend.

"Wouldn't it be *heavenly*, Marguerite, to be engaged—you and I?" she said, in a tone of dreamy rapture. "To have a dark, handsome man with proud black eyes just dying with love for you, going down on his knees, and giving you presents, and taking you out and all—oh, Marguerite, just think of it!"

Meg's eyes looked wistful. "We're not old enough, though, yet," she said with a sigh.

Aldith tossed her head. "That's nonsense; why, Clara Allison is only seventeen, and look at your own stepmother. Plenty of girls are actually *married* at sixteen, Marguerite, and a man proposed to my sister Beatrice when she was only fifteen."

Meg looked impressed and thoughtful.

Then Aldith rose to go. "Mind you're in time for the boat to-morrow," she said, as they reached

the gate; "and, Marguerite, be *sure* you make yourself look very nice—wear your cornflower dress—
and see if Mrs. Woolcot will lend you a pair of her
gloves, your grey ones are just a little shabby, aren't
they, dear?"

"H'm," said Meg, colouring.

"And Mr. James Graham always comes back on
that boat, and the two Courtney boys—Andrew
Courtney told Beatrice he thought you seemed a
nice little thing; he often notices you, he says,
because you blush so."

"I can't help it," Meg said, unhappily. "Aldith,
how ought the ribbon to go on my hat? I'm going
to retrim it again."

"Oh, square bows, somewhat stiff, and well at the
side," the oracle said. "I'm glad you're going to,
dear, it looked just a wee bit dowdy, didn't it?"

Meg coloured again.

"Have you done your French?" she said, as she
pulled open the gate.

"In a way," Aldith said carelessly. Then she put
up her chin. "Those frowzy-looking Smiths always
make a point of having no mistakes; and Janet
Green, whose hats are always four seasons behind
the fashions; I prefer to have a few errors, just to
show I haven't to work hard and be a teacher after
I——"

But just here she stumbled and fell down her full
length in a most undignified manner, right across
the muddy sidewalk.

It was a piece of string and Baby's vengeance.

CHAPTER 7

"What Say You to Falling in Love?"

MEG WAS LOOKING ILL, there was no doubt about it. Her pretty pink-and-white complexion was losing its fresh look, a slightly irritable expression had settled round a mouth that a few months back had seemed made for smiles only. And, terribly unromantic fact, her nose was quite florid-looking at times. Now a heroine may have the largest, deepest, and most heavily lashed eyes imaginable; she may have hair in very truth like the gold "mown from a harvest's middle floor"; she may have lips like cherries and teeth like pearls, and a red nose will be so utterly fatal that all these other charms will pass unnoticed. It cost Meg real anguish of spirit. She carefully read all the Answers to Correspondents in the various papers Aldith lent her in search of a remedy, but nearly everyone seemed to be asking for recipes to promote the growth of the eyelashes or to prevent *embonpoint*. Not one she chanced on said, "A red nose in a girl is generally caused by indigestion or *tight-lacing*." She asked Aldith to suggest something, and that young person thought that vaseline and sulphur mixed together, and spread over the afflicted member, would have the desired effect. So every night Meg fastened her bedroom door with a wedge of wood, keys being unknown luxuries at Misrule, and anointed her poor little nose most carefully with the greasy mixture, lying all night on her back to prevent it rubbing off on the pillow.

Once Pip had forced his way in to demand a few stitches for his braces which had split, and she had been compelled to wrap her whole face hastily up in a towel and declare she had violent neuralgia, and he must go to Esther or one of the servants. Had he seen and known the cause there would have been no end to the teasing.

Nowadays Meg spent a great deal of time in her bedroom, that she had all to herself while Judy was away. In its privacy she trimmed and retrimmed her hats, altered her dresses, read her novels, and sat in front of the looking-glass with her hair down, dreaming of being quite grown up and in love. For just now both to Aldith and herself that state of life seemed the only one altogether lovely and desirable. Meg used to curl herself up in a big easy-chair that had drifted to her room because its springs were broken, and dream long, beautiful, hopeless dreams of a lover with "long black lashes and a soldierly carriage." Of course it was highly reprehensible to have such thoughts at the tender age of sixteen, but then the child had no mother to check that erring imagination, and she was a daughter of the South.

Australian girls nearly always begin to think of "lovers and nonsense," as middlefolks call it, long before their English aged sisters do. While still in

64

the short-frock period of existence, and while their hair is still free-flowing, they take the keenest interest in boys—boys of neighbouring schools, other girls' brothers, young bank clerks, and the like. Not because they would be good playmates, but because they look at them in the light of possible "sweethearts." I do not say English girl children are free from this. By no means; in every school there may be found one or two this way inclined, giggling, forward young things who want whipping and sending to play cricket or dolls again. But in this land of youthfulness it is the rule more frequently than the exception, and herein lies the chief defect of the very young Australian girl. She is like a peach, a beautiful, smooth, rich peach, that has come to ripeness almost in a day, and that hastens to rub off the soft, delicate bloom that is its chief charm, just to show its bright, warm colouring more clearly. Aldith had, to her own infinite satisfaction, brushed away her own "bloom," and was at present busily engaged in trying to remove Meg's, which was very soft and lovely before she touched it. The novels had taken away a little, and the "Block" a little more, but Meg was naturally fresh-minded, and it took time to make much difference. Just now, under her friend's tutelage, she was being inducted into the delightful mysteries of sweet-hearting, and for the time it quite filled her somewhat purposeless young life. But it all ended with an adventure that years afterwards used to make her cheeks tingle painfully at the thought.

After the bi-weekly French lesson, as I have said, the two friends used to come back together in the river-boat at five o'clock. And by this boat there always came two boys by the name of Courtney, and a third boy, Aldith's particular property, James Graham. Now the young people had become known to each other at picnics and the like in the neighbourhood, but the acquaintance, instead of ripening on frequent meeting into a frank, pleasant friendship, had taken the turn of secrecy and silly playing at love. James Graham was in a lawyer's office, a young articled clerk of seventeen in undue haste to be that delightful thing, a man. He carried a cane, and was very particular about his hat and necktie and his boots, which generally were tan. And he had the faintest possible moustache, that he caressed with great frequency, and that privately Aldith thought adorable. Aldith's pert, sprightly manner pleased him, and in a very short time they had got to the period of passing notes into each other's hands and sighing sentimentally. Not that the notes contained much harm, they were generally of rather a formal character.

" MY DEAR MISS MACCARTHY," one would run— " Why were you not on the boat yesterday? I looked for you till it was no use looking longer, and then the journey was blank. How charmingly that big hat suits you, and those jonquils at your neck. Might I beg one of the flowers? just one, please, Aldith.

Your devoted friend,
JAMES GRAHAM."

And Aldith's, written on a sheet of her note-book

with a pink programme pencil that she always kept in her purse, might be no worse than:

"DEAR MR. GRAHAM,

"What *ever* can you want these flowers at my neck for? They have been there all day, and are dead and spoiled. I can't *imagine* what good they'll be to you. Still, of course, if you *really* care for them you shall have them. I am *so* glad you like this hat. I shall always like it *now*. Did you *really* miss me yesterday? I had gone to have my photo taken. Marguerite thinks it very good indeed, but I am *sure* it flatters me *too* much.

Yours truly,

L. ALDITH EVELYN MACCARTHY."

Now Mr. James Graham had a great friend in one of the before-mentioned Courtney boys, Andrew by name. He was a handsome lad of eighteen, still a schoolboy, but possessed of fascinating manners and a pair of really beautiful eyes.

And since his friend and companion Jim had taken to "having fun" with "the girl MacCarthy," he objected to being left out in the cold. So he began to pay marked attentions to Meg, who blushed right up to her soft, pretty fringe every time he spoke to her, and looked painfully conscious and guilty if he said anything at all complimentary to her.

The other boy, Alan Courtney, was very tall and broad-shouldered, and not at all good-looking. He had a strong, plain face, grey eyes deeply set, and brown hair that looked as if he was in a constant state of rumpling it up the wrong way. He was a University student, and a great footballer, and he never diverted himself on the long homeward journey in the way Andrew and his friend did.

He used generally to give a half-contemptuous nod as he passed the little group, uncovering his head for the shortest possible period consistent with civility, and making his way to the far end of the boat. One time as he passed them Aldith was drooping her lashes and using her eyes with great effect, and Meg was almost positive she heard him mutter under his breath, "Silly young fools!" He used to smoke at his end of the boat—cigars at the beginning of term and a short, black, villainous-looking pipe at the end—and Meg used secretly to think how manly he looked, and to sigh profoundly.

For I may as well tell you now as later what this foolish little thing had done after a few months' course of Aldith and novels. She had fallen in love as nearly as it is possible for sweet sixteen to do; and it was with Alan, who had no good looks nor pleasant manners—not Andrew, who had speaking eyes, and curls that "made his forehead like the rising sun"; not Andrew, who gave her tender glances and con-versation peppermints that said "My heart is thine," but Alan, who took no notice whatever of her beyond an occasional half-scornful bow.

Poor little Meg! She was very miserable in these days, and yet it was a kind of exquisite misery that she hugged to her to keep it warm. No one guessed her secret. She would have died rather than allow even Aldith to get a suspicion of it, and accepted Andrew's notes and smiles as if there was nothing more she wanted. But she grew a trifle thin and large-eyed, and used to make copious notes in her diary every night, and to write a truly appalling quantity of verses, in which "heart" and "part," "grieve" and "leave," "weep" and "keep," and "sigh" and "die," were most often the concluding words of the lines. She endured Andrew for several reasons. He was Alan's brother for one thing, and was always saying things about "old Al," and recording his prowess on the football field; and Aldith might discover her secret if she gave him the cold shoulder altogether. Besides this, Andrew had the longest eyelashes she had ever seen, and she must have *somebody* to say pretty things to her, even if it was not the person she would have wished it to be.

One day things came to a crisis.

"No more trips on the dear old boat for a month," Aldith remarked, from her corner of the cabin.

"This is appalling! Whatever do you mean, Miss MacCarthy?" James Graham said, with exaggerated despair in his voice.

"Monsieur H—— has given the class a month's holiday. He is going to Melbourne," Aldith returned, with a sigh.

Meg echoed it as in duty bound, and Andrew said fiercely that hanging was too good for Monsieur H——. What did he mean by such inhuman conduct, he should like to know; and however were Jim and himself to maintain life in the meantime?

It was James who speedily thought of "a way out."

"Couldn't we go for a walk somewhere one evening—just we four?" he said insinuatingly.

Aldith and Andrew thought the proposal a brilliant one; and though Meg had at first shaken her head decidedly, in the end she was prevailed upon, and promised faithfully to go.

They were to meet in a bush paddock adjoining the far one belonging to Misrule, to walk for about an hour, returning by half-past seven, before it grew dusk.

"I am going to ask you for something that day, Meg," Andrew whispered just as they were parting. "I wonder if I shall get it."

Meg flushed in her nervous, conscious way, and wondered to herself for a moment whether he intended to ask for a lock of her hair, a thing Jim Graham had already obtained from Aldith.

"What?" she said unwillingly.

"A kiss," he whispered.

The next minute the others had joined them, and there was no chance for the indignant answer that trembled on her lips. She had even to shake hands, to appear as if nothing had happened, and to part apparently good friends.

"Half-past six sharp, Marguerite. I will never forgive you if you don't come," Aldith said, as they parted at her gate.

"I—you—— Oh, Aldith, I don't see how I *can* come," Meg faltered, the crimson in her cheeks again. "I've never done anything like it before. I'm sure it's not right."

But the curl in Aldith's lip made her ashamed of herself.

70

"You're just twelve, Marguerite," the young lady said calmly: "you're not a bit more than twelve. You'd better get a roll again, and a picture-book with morals. I'll ask Andrew to buy you one and a bit of cord, too, to tie you in your high chair in the nursery."

Such sarcasm was too much for Meg. She promised hastily and unconditionally to be on the spot at the time mentioned, and fled away up the path to obey the summons of the wildly clanging tea-bell.

But for the two intervening days her secret hung upon her like a burden of guilt, and she longed inexpressibly for a confidante who would advise her what to do at this distressing issue. Not Judy: that young person was too downright, too sensible, too much of a child and a boy—she would never dare to tell her anything of the sort. She could fancy the scorn in her sister's large clear eyes, the ringing laughter such a tale would evoke, the scathing, clever ridicule that would fall on her shrinking shoulders. Not Esther: her very position as step-mother precluded such an idea, and, besides that, the General's gums were gradually disclosing wee white double pearls, and his health thereby was affected, and causing her too much anxiety to allow her to notice Meg's oppression of mind.

By the night decided upon, the child had worked herself up into a strong state of excitement.

Half-past six was the time settled upon, and, as she knew, it was broad daylight even then. She felt she really dare not, could not go. Suppose her father or Esther, some of her scornful young sisters or brothers, should be about and see the meeting, or any of the neighbours—why, she could never survive the shame of it! Yet go she must, or Aldith would despise her. Besides, she had made up her mind fully to tell Andrew plainly she could not allow him to talk to her as he had been doing. After that last terrible whisper, she felt it necessary that she should let him understand clearly that she did not approve of his conduct, and would be "his friend," but nothing more.

But why had they not thought of deciding on an hour when it would be darker? she kept saying to herself: there would be no danger of being seen then; she could slip out of the house without any difficulty, and run through the paddocks under cover of the kindly dusk; whereas if it was light, and she tried to creep away, at least two or three of the children would fly after her and offer generously to "come too."

At last, too afraid to go in the light, and unwilling for Aldith to reproach her for not going at all, she did in her excitement and desperation a thing so questionable that for long after she could not think of it without horror.

"DEAR MR. COURTNEY," she wrote, sitting down at her dressing-table, and scribbling away hurriedly in pencil:

"It would be horrid going for the walk so early. Let us go later, when it is quite dark. It will be *ever* so much nicer, for no one will be able to see us. And let us meet at the end of the paddocks where the bush grows thickly, it will be more private. I am writing to Aldith to tell her to go at that time, she will tell Mr. Graham.

Yours sincerely,

M. WOOLCOT.

"P.S.—I must ask you, please, not to kiss me. I should be very angry indeed if you did. I don't like kissing at all."

She wrote the last paragraph in a nervous hurry for she had a dread that he might fulfil his promise, if she did not forbid him as soon as they met. Then she slipped it into an envelope and addressed it to A. Courtney, Esq., it never having even occurred to her for a moment that there was anything at all strange or unconventional in a young girl making such a point that the meeting should be in the dark.

Next she wrote a few lines of explanation to Aldith, and told her to be sure to be in the paddock by half-past eight, and she (Meg) would slip out when the children were going to bed and unlikely to notice.

And then she went out into the garden to find messengers for her two notes. Little Flossie Courtney had been spending the afternoon with Nellie, and Meg called her back from the gate just as she was going home, and, unseen by the children, entrusted the note to her.

"Give it to your brother Andrew the minute he comes from school," she whispered, popping a big chocolate at the same time into the little girl's mouth. Bunty was next bribed, with a promise of the same melting delicacies, to run up to Aldith's with the other letter, and Meg breathed freely again, feeling she had skilfully averted the threatening danger attendant on the evening meeting.

But surely the notes were fated! Bunty delivered his safely enough to the housemaid at the Mac-Carthys', and in answer to the girl's question "s'posed there was an answer, girls always 'spected one to nothing."

Aldith was confined to her room with a sudden severe cold, and wrote a note to her friend, telling her how she was too ill to be allowed out, and had written to Mr. Graham, and Mr. Courtney, too, postponing the walk for a week.

Now this note, in its pale pink triangular envelope, was transferred to Bunty's pocket among his marbles and peanuts and string. And, as might be expected, he fell in with some other choice spirits on the return journey, and was soon on his knees by the roadside playing marbles.

He lost ten, exclusive of his best agate, fought a boy who had unlawfully possessed himself of his most cherished "conny," and returned home with saddened spirits an hour later, only to find as he went through the gate that he had lost Aldith's dainty little note.

Now Meg had promised him eight chocolate walnuts on his return, and if this same boy had one weakness more pronounced than others, it was his extreme partiality for this kind of confectionery, and he had not tasted one for weeks, so no wonder it almost broke his heart to think they would be forfeited.

"I know she'll be stingy enough to say I haven't

earned them, just 'cause I dropped that girl's stupid letter," he said to himself, miserably, "and I don't suppose there was anything in it but 'Dearest Marguerite, let us always tell each other our secrets'; I heard her say that twice, and of course she writes it, too." Then temptation came upon him swiftly, suddenly.

By nature Bunty was the most arrant little story-teller ever born, and it was only Judy's fearless honesty and strongly expressed scorn for equivocation that had kept him moderately truthful. But Judy was miles away, and could not possibly wither him up with her look of utter contempt. He was at the nursery door now, turning the handle with hesitating hands.

"What a time you've been," said Meg from the table, where she was mending a boxful of her gloves. "Well, what did she say?"

Just at her elbow was the gay *bonbonnière* containing the brown, cream-encrusted walnuts.

"She said, 'All right,'" said Bunty gruffly.

Meg counted the eight chocolates out into his little grimy hand, and resumed her mending with a relieved sigh. And Bunty, with a defiant, shamed look in his eyes, stuffed the whole of the sweets into his mouth at once, as if to preclude the possibility of a sudden repentance.

The other note was equally unfortunate. Little Flossie went home, her thoughts intent upon a certain Grannie bonnet Nell had promised to make for her new doll.

"Gween with pink stwings," she was saying softly to herself as she climbed the steps to her own door.

75

Alan was lying on the veranda lounge, smoking his black pipe.

"Gween what?" he laughed—"guinea-pigs or kangaroos?"

"Clawice Maud's bonnet," the little girl said, and entered forthwith into a grave discussion with him as to the colour he thought more suitable for that waxen lady's winter cloak.

Then she turned to go in.

"What's that sticking out of your wee pocket, Flossie girl?" he said, as she brushed past him.

She stopped a second and felt.

"Oh, nearly I didn't wemember, an' I pwomised I would—it's a letter for you, Alan," she said, and gave Meg's poor little epistle up into the very hands of the Philistine.

CHAPTER 8

A Catapult and a Catastrophe

❦

"Oh, sweet pale Margaret,
Oh, rare pale Margaret,
What lit your eyes with tearful power?"

THE DUSK HAD FALLEN very softly and tenderly
over the garden, and the paddocks, and the river.
There was just the faintest wind at the water's edge,
but it seemed almost too tired after the hot, long
day to breathe and make ripples. Very slowly the
grey, still light deepened, and a white star or two
came out and blinked up away in the high, far
heavens. Down behind the gum trees, across the
river, there was a still whiter moon; a stretch of
water near was beginning to smile up to it. Meg
hoped it would not climb past the tree-tops before
eight o'clock, or the long paddocks would be flooded
with light and she would be seen. At tea-time, and
during the early part of the evening, she was pre-
occupied and inclined to be irritable in her anxiety,
and she snubbed Bunty two or three times quite
unkindly.

He had been hovering about her ever since six
o'clock in almost a pitiable way.

It was characteristic of this small boy that when

77

he had been tempted into departing from the paths of truth he was absolutely wretched until he had confessed, and rubbed his little unclean hands into his wet eyes until he was "a sight to dream of, not to tell."

Pip said it was because he was a coward, and had not the moral courage to go to sleep with a lie on his soul, for fear he might wake up and see an angel with a fiery sword standing by his bedside. And I must sorrowfully acknowledge this seemed a truer view of the case than believing the boy was really impressed with the heinousness of his offence and anxious to make amends. For the very next day, if occasion sufficiently strong offered, he would fall again, and the very next night would creep up to somebody and whimper, with his knuckles in his eyes, that he had "t—t—told a s—s—story, boo— hoo!"

By seven o'clock this particular evening he was miserably repentant; several tears had trickled down his cheeks and mingled with the ink of the map he was engaged upon for Miss Marsh. He established himself at Meg's elbow, and kept looking up into her face in a yearning love-and-forgive-me kind of way that she found infinitely embarrassing; for she had begun to suspect, from his strange con- duct, that he had in some way learned the con- tents of her note, and was trying to discourage her from her enterprise. The more he gazed at her the redder and more uncomfortable she became.

"You can have my new c—c—catapult," he whis- pered once, giving her a tearful, imploring look, that she interpreted as an entreaty to stay safely at home.

At last the clock had travelled up to eight, and the children being engaged in a wordy warfare over the possession of a certain stray dog that had come to Misrule in the afternoon, she slipped out of the room unobserved. No one was in the hall, and she picked up the becoming, fleecy cloud she had hidden there, twisted it round her head, and crept out of the side door and along the first path.

Down in the garden the ground was white with fallen rose leaves, and the air full of their dying breath; a clump of pampas grass stood tall and soft against the sky; some native trees, left growing among the cultivated shrubs, stretched silver-white arms up to the moon and gave the little hurrying figure a ghostly kind of feeling. Out of the gate and into the first paddock, where the rose scent did not come at all, and only a pungent smell of wattle was in the thin, hushed air. More gum trees, and more white, ghostly arms; then a sharp movement near the fence, a thick, sepulchral whisper, and a stifled scream from Meg.

" Here's the c—c—c—catapult, M—Meg; t—take it," Bunty said, his face white and miserable.

"You little stupid! What do you mean coming creeping here like this? " Meg said, angry as soon as her heart began to beat again.

"I only w—wanted to p—p—please you, M— M—Meggie," the little boy said, with a bitter sob in his voice.

He had put both his arms round her waist, and

79

was burying his nose in her white muslin dress. She shook him off hastily.

"All right; there—thanks," she said. "Now go home, Bunty; I want to have a quiet walk in the moonlight by myself."

He screwed his knuckles as far into his eyes as they would go, his mouth opened, and his lower lip dropped down, down.

"I t—t—told y—y—you a b—b—big st—st—story," he wept, rocking to and fro where he stood.

"Did you? Oh, all right! Now go home," she said impatiently. "You always *are* telling stories, Bunty, you know, so I'm not surprised. There go along."

"But—but I'm—must tell you all ab—ab—about it," he said, still engaged in driving his eyes into his head.

"No, you needn't; I'll forgive you this time," she said magnanimously, "only don't do it again. Now run away at once, or you won't have your map done, and Miss Marsh will punish you."

His eyes returned to their proper position, likewise his hands. His heart was perfectly light again as he turned to go back to the house. When he had gone a few steps he came back.

"D'ye want that catapult very much, Meg?" he said gently. "You're only a girl, so I don't 'spect it would be very much good to you, would it?"

"No, I don't want it. Here, take it, and hurry back: think of your map," Meg returned, in a very fever of impatience at his slowness.

And then Bunty, utterly happy once more,

turned and ran away gaily up to the house.

And Meg let down the slip-rail, put it back in its place with trembling fingers, and fled in wild haste through the two remaining paddocks.

The wattle-scrub at the end was very quiet; there was not a rustle, not a sound of a voice, not a sound of the affected little laugh that generally told when Aldith was near.

Meg stopped breathless, and peered among the bushes; there was a tall figure leaning against the fence.

"Andrew!" she said in a sharp whisper, and forgetting in her anxiety that she never called him by his Christian name—"where are the others? Hasn't Aldith come?"

There was the smell of a cigar, and, looking closely, she saw to her horror it was Alan.

"Oh!" she said, in an indescribable tone.

Her heart gave one frightened, shamed bound, and then seemed to stop beating altogether.

She looked up at him as if entreating him not to have too bad an opinion of her; but his face wore the contemptuous look she had grown to dread and his lips were finely curled.

"I—I only came out for a little walk; it is such a beautiful evening," she said, with miserable lameness; and then in a tone of justification she added, "it's my father's paddock, too."

He leaned back against the fence and looked down at her.

"Flossie gave me your note, and as it seemed addressed to me, and I was told it was for me, I opened it," he said.

F   81

"You *knew* it was for Andrew," she said—not looking at him, however.

"So I presumed when I had read it," he returned slowly; "but Andrew has not come back to-night yet, so I came instead; it's all the same as long as it's a boy, isn't it?"

The girl made no reply, only put her hand up and drew the cloud more closely round her head.

His lips curled a little more.

"And I know how to kiss, too, I assure you. I am quite a good hand at it, though you may not think so. Oh yes, I know you *said* you did not want to be kissed; but then, girls always say that, don't they?—even when they expect it most."

Still Meg did not speak, and the calm, merciless voice went on:

"I am afraid it is hardly dark enough for you, is it? The moon is very much in the way, do you not think so? Still, perhaps we can find a darker place farther on, and then I can kiss you without danger. What is the matter?—are you always as quiet as this with Andrew?"

"Oh, *don't!*" said Meg, in a choking voice.

The mocking tone died instantly out of his voice.

"Miss Meg, you used to seem such a nice little girl," he said quietly; "what have you let that horrid MacCarthy girl spoil you for? For she *is* horrid, though you may not think so."

Meg did not speak or move, and he went on with a gentle earnestness that she had not thought him capable of.

"I have watched her on the boat, systematically

going to work to spoil you, and can't help thinking of the pity of it. I imagined how I should feel if my little sister Flossie ever fell in with such a girl, and began to flirt and make herself conspicuous, and I wondered would you mind if I spoke to you about it. Are you very angry with me, Miss Meg?"

But Meg leaned her head against the rough fence and began to sob—little, dry, heartbroken sobs that went to the boy's warm heart.

"I oughtn't to have spoken as I did at first—I was a perfect brute," he said remorsefully; "forgive me, won't you? Please, little Miss Meg—I would rather cut my hand off than really hurt you."

This last was a little consoling, at any rate, and Meg lifted her face half a second, white and pathetic in the moonlight, and all wet with grievous tears.

"I—I—oh! indeed I have not been quite so horrid as you think," she said brokenly; "I didn't want to come this walk—and 'oh! indeed, indeed, indeed I wouldn't allow *anyone* to kiss me. Oh, *please* do believe me!"

"I do, I do indeed," he said eagerly; "I only said it because—well, because I am a great rough brute, and don't know how to talk to a little, tender girl. Dear Miss Meg, do shake hands and tell me you forgive my boorishness."

Meg extended a small white hand, and he shook it warmly. Then they walked up the paddocks together, and parted at a broken gate leading into the garden.

"I'll never flirt again while I live," she said with

83

great earnestness, as he bade her good-bye; and he answered encouragingly, " No, I am quite sure you won't—leave it to girls like Aldith, won't you? you only wanted to be set straight. Good-bye, little Miss Meg."

CHAPTER 9

Consequences

───────── ❈ ─────────

"However could you do it?
Some day, no doubt, you'll rue it!"

MEG'S TROUBLES WERE NOT QUITE OVER, however, even yet. When she got into the house Nellie met her in the hall and stared at her.

"Where *have* you been?" she said, a slow wonder in her round eyes. "I've been hunting and hunting for you."

"What for?" said Meg shortly.

"Oh, Dr. Gormeston and Mrs. Gormeston and two Miss Gormestons are in the drawing-room, and I think they'll stay for ever and ever."

"Well?" said Meg.

"And the General is ill again, and Esther says she won't leave him for a second, not if Gog and Magog were down there dying to see her."

"Well?" said Meg again.

"And Father is as mad as he can be, and is having to keep them all amused himself. He's sung 'My sweetheart when a boy' and 'Mona,' and he's told them all about his horses, and now I s'pose he doesn't know what to do."

"Well, I can't help it," Meg said wearily, and as if the subject had no interest for her.

"But you'll just have to!" Nell cried sharply. "I've done my best: he sent out and said we girls were to go in, and you weren't anywhere, so there was only Baby and me."

"And what did you do?" Meg asked, curious in spite of herself.

"Oh, Baby talked to Miss Gormeston, and they asked me to play," she returned, "so I played the 'Keel Row.' Only I forgot till I had finished that it was in two sharps," she added sadly. "And then Baby told Mrs. Gormeston all about Judy leaving the General at the Barracks, and being sent to boarding school for it, and about the green frog Bunty gave her, and then Father said we'd better go to bed, and asked why ever you didn't come in."

"I'll go, I'll go," Meg said hastily, "he'll be fearfully cross to-morrow about it. Oh! and, Nell, go and tell Martha to send in the wine and biscuits and things in half an hour."

She flung off her cloud, smoothed her ruffled hair, and peeped in the hall-stand glass to see if the night wind had taken away the traces of her recent tears.

Then she went into the drawing-room, where her father was looking quite heated and unhappy over his efforts to entertain four guests who were of the class popularly known as "heavy in hand."

"Play something, Meg," he said presently, when the greetings were finished, and a silence seemed settling down over them all again; "or sing something, that will be better—haven't you anything you can sing?"

Now Meg on ordinary occasions had a pleasant, fresh little voice of her own, that could be listened to with a certain amount of pleasure, but this evening she was tired and excited and unhappy. She sang "Within a mile of Edinboro' town," and was exceedingly flat all through.

She knew her father was sitting on edge all the time, and that her mistakes were grating on him, and at the end of the song, rather than turn round immediately and face them all, she began to play Kowalski's March Hongroise. But the keys seemed to be rising up and hitting her hands, and the piano was growing unsteady, and rocking to and fro in an alarming manner; she made a horrible jangle as she clutched at the music-holder for safety, and the next minute swayed from the stool and fell in a dead faint right into Dr. Gormeston's arms, providentially extended just in time.

The heavy, heated atmosphere had proved too much for her in her unhinged state of mind.

Captain Woolcot was extraordinarily upset by the occurrence; not one of his children had ever done such a thing before, and as Meg lay on the sofa, with her little fair head drooping against the red frilled cushions, her face white and unconscious, she looked strangely like her mother, whom he had buried out in the churchyard four years ago. He went to the filter for a glass of water, and, as it trickled, wondered in a dull, mechanical kind of way if his little dead wife thought he had been too quick in appointing Esther to her kingdom. And then, as he stood near the sofa and looked at the death-like face, he wondered with a cold chill at his heart whether Meg was going to die, too, and if so would she be able to tell the same little wife that Esther received more tenderness at his hands than she had done.

His reverie was interrupted by the doctor's sharp, surprised voice. He was talking to Esther, who had been hastily summoned to the scene, and who had helped to unfasten the pretty bodice.

"Why, the child is tight-laced!" he said; "surely you must have noticed it, madam. That pressure, if it has been constant, has been enough to half kill her. Chut, chut! faint indeed—I wonder she has not taken fits or gone into a decline before this."

Then a cloud of trouble came over Esther's beautiful face—she had failed again in her duty. Her husband was regarding her almost gloomily from the sofa, where the little figure lay in its crumpled muslin dress, and her heart told her these children were not receiving a mother's care at her hands.

Afterwards, when Meg was safely in bed and the excitement all over, she went up to her husband almost timidly.

"I'm only twenty, Jack; don't be too hard on me!" she said with a little sob in her voice. "I *can't* be all to them that *she* was, can I?"

He kissed the bright, beautiful head against his shoulder, and comforted her with a tender word or two. But again and again that night there came to him Meg's white, still face as it lay on the scarlet cushions, and he knew the wind that stirred the curtains at the window had been playing with the long grass in the churchyard a few minutes since.

CHAPTER 10

Bunty in the Light of a Hero

> " 'I know him to be valiant.'
> 'I was told that by one that knows him better than you.'
> 'What's he?'
> 'Marry, he told me so himself, and he said he cared not who
> knew it.' "

BUNTY HAD BEEN BETRAYED into telling another story. It was a very big one, and he was proportionately miserable. Everyone else had gone out but Meg, who was still in bed after her fainting-fit, and he had been having a lonely game of cricket down in the paddock by himself. But even with a brand-new cricket ball this game palls after a time when one has to bowl and bat and backstop in solitary state. So presently he put his bat over into the garden, and began to throw the ball about in an aimless fashion, while he cogitated on what he should do next. His father's hack was standing away at the farther end of the paddock, and in an idle, thoughtless way Bunty sauntered down towards it, and then sent his ball spinning over the ground in its direction "to give it a jump." Nothing was further from his thoughts than an idea of hurting

89

the animal, and when the ball struck it full on the leg, and it moved away limping, he hastened down to it, white and anxious.

He could see he had done serious mischief by the way the poor thing held its leg up from the ground and quivered when he touched it. Terror seized him forthwith, and he turned hastily round with his usual idea of hiding in his head. But to his utter dismay, when he got half-way back across the paddock he saw his father and a brother officer come out of the wicket gate leading from the garden and saunter slowly down in the direction of the horse, which was a valuable and beautiful one.

In terror at what he had done, he slipped the cricket ball into the front of his sailor jacket, and, falling hurriedly upon his knees, began playing an absorbing game of marbles. His trembling thumb had hit about a dozen at random when he heard his name called in stentorian tones.

He rose, brushed the dust from his shaking knees, and walked slowly down to his father.

"Go and tell Pat I want him instantly," the Captain said. He had the horse's leg in his hand and was examining it anxiously. "If he's not about, send Pip. I can't think how it's happened—do you know anything of this, Bunty?"

"No, of course not! I n—never did n—n—nothing," Bunty said with chattering teeth, but his father was too occupied to notice his evident guilt, and bade him go at once.

So he went up to the stables and sent Pat posthaste back to his father.

And then he stole into the house, purloined two

apples and a bit of cake from the dining-room, and went away to be utterly miserable until he had confessed.

He crept into a disused shed some distance from the house; in days gone by it had been a stable, and had a double loft over it that was only to be reached by a ladder in the last stage of dilapidation. Bunty scrambled up, sat down in an unhappy little heap among some straw, and began thoughtfully to gnaw an apple.

If ever a little lad was in need of a wise, loving, motherly mother it was this same dirty-faced, heavy-hearted one who sat with his small rough head against a cobwebby beam and muttered dejectedly, "'Twasn't my fault. 'Twas the horse."

He fancied something moved in the second loft, which was divided from the one he was in by a low partition. "Shoo—shoo, get away!" he called, thinking it was rats. He struck the floor several times with his heavy little boots.

"Shoo!" he said.

"Bunty."

The boy turned pale to his lips. That odd, low whisper of his name, that strange rustle so near him —oh, what *could* it mean?

"Bunty."

Again the name sounded. Louder this time, but in a tired voice, that struck him some way with a strange thrill. The rustling grew louder, something was getting over the partition, crossing the floor, coming towards him. He gave a sob of terror and flung himself face downwards on the ground, hiding his little blanched face among the straw.

91

"Bunty," said the voice again, and a light hand touched his arm.

"Help me—*help* me!" he shrieked. "Meg—oh! Father—Esther!"

But one hand was hastily put over his mouth and another pulled him into a sitting position.

He had shut his eyes very tightly, so as not to see the ghostly visitant that he knew had come to punish him for his sin. But something made him open them, and then he felt he could never close them again for amazement.

For it was Judy's hand that was over his mouth, and Judy's self that was standing beside him.

"My golly!" he said, in a tone of stupefaction. He stared hard at her to make sure she was real flesh and blood. "How*ever* did you get here?"

But Judy made no answer. She merely took the remaining apple and cake from his hand, and, sitting down, devoured them in silence.

"Haven't you got any more?" she said anxiously.

Then he noticed what a tall, gaunt, strange-looking Judy it was. Her clothes were hanging round her almost in tatters, her boots were burst and white with dust, her brown face was thin and sharp, and her hair matted and rough.

"My golly!" the little boy said again, his eyes threatening to start out of his head—"my golly, Judy, what have you been doin'?"

"I—I've run away, Bunty," Judy said, in a quavering voice. "I've walked all the way from school. I wanted to see you all so badly."

"My jiggery!" Bunty said.

"I've thought it all out," Judy continued,

92

pushing back her hair in a weary way. "I can't quite remember everything just now, I am so tired, but everything will be all right."

"But what'll he say?" Bunty said with frightened eyes, as a vision of his father crossed his mind.

"He won't know, of course," Judy returned, in a matter-of-fact manner. "I shall just live here in this loft for a time, and you can all come to see me and bring me food and things, and then presently I'll go back to school." She sank down among the straw and shut her eyes in an exhausted way for a minute or two, and Bunty watched her half fascinated.

"How far is it from your school?" he said at last.

"Seventy-seven miles." Judy shuddered a little. "I got a lift in a luggage train from Lawson to Springwood, and a ride in a cart for a little way, but I walked the rest. I've been nearly a week coming," she added after a pause, and shut her eyes again for quite a long time. Then a tear or two of weakness and self-pity trickled from beneath her black lashes, and made a little clean mark down her cheeks. Bunty's throat swelled at the sight of them, he had never seen Judy cry as long as he could remember. He patted her thin hand, he rubbed his head against her shoulder, and said, "Never mind, old girl," in a thick voice.

But that brought half a dozen great heavy drops hurrying down from beneath the closed lashes, and the girl turned over and lay face downwards to hide them. Then she struggled up to a sitting position and actually began to laugh.

"*If* the Miss Burtons could see me!" she said. "Oh, I've managed everything *so* beautifully; they

93

think I'm spending a fortnight at Katoomba—oh, *Bunty*, you ought to see the curls Miss Marian Burton wears plastered at each side of her cheeks!" She broke off, laughing almost hysterically, and then coughing till the tears came back in her eyes.

"Do go and get me something to eat," she said crossly, when she got her breath—"you might remember I've had nothing to eat since yesterday morning; only you always were selfish, Bunty."

He got up and moved away in a great hurry. "What could you eat? what shall I get?" he said, and put one leg down the trap-door.

"Anything so long as it's a lot," she said—"*anything!* I feel I could eat this straw, and crunch up the beams as if they were biscuits. I declare I've had to keep my eyes off you, Bunty; you're so fat I keep longing to pick your bones."

Her eyes shone with a spark of their old fun, but then she began to cough again, and, after the paroxysm had passed, lay back exhausted.

"Do fetch some of the others," she called faintly, as his head was disappearing. "You're not much good alone, you know."

His head bobbed back a moment, and he tried to smile away the pain her words gave him, for just at that minute he would have died for her without a murmur.

"I'm awf'ly sorry, Judy," he said gently, "but the others are all out. Wouldn't I do? I'd do anything, Judy—please."

Judy disregarded the little sniffle that accompanied the last words, and turned her face to the wall.

Two big tears trickled down again.

"They *might* have stayed in," she said with a sob. "They might have known I should try to come. Where are they?"

"Pip's gone fishing," he said, "and Nell's carrying the basket for him. And Baby's at the Courtneys', and Esther's gone to town with the General. Oh, and Meg's ill in bed, because her stays were too tight last night and she fainted."

"I suppose they haven't missed me a scrap," was her bitter thought, when she heard how everything seemed going on as usual, while she had been living through so much just to see them all.

Then the odd feeling of faintness came back, and she closed her eyes again and lay motionless, forgetful of time, place, or hunger.

Bunty sped across the paddock on winged feet; the sight of his father near the stables gave him a momentary shock, and brought his own trouble to mind, but he shook it off again and hurried on. The pantry door was locked. Martha, the cook, kept it in that condition generally on account of his own sinful propensities for making away with her tarts and cakes; it was only by skilful stratagem he could ever get in, as he remembered dejectedly.

But Judy's hunger! Nothing to eat since yesterday morning!

He remembered, with a feeling of pain even now, the horrible sinking sensation he had experienced last week when for punishment he had been sent to bed without his tea. And Judy had forgone three meals! He shut his lips tightly, and a light of almost heroic resolve came into his eyes. Round at the side of the house was the window to the pantry; he had often gazed longingly up at it, but had never ventured to attempt the ascent, for there was a horrible cactus creeper up the wall.

But now for Judy's sake he would do it or die.

He marched round the house and up to the side window; no one was about, the whole place seemed very quiet. Martha, as he had seen, was cooking in the kitchen, and the other girl was whitening the front veranda. He gave one steady look at the great spiky thorns, and the next minute was climbing up among them.

Oh, how they pierced and tore him! There was a great jagged wound up one arm, his left stocking was ripped away and a deep red scratch showed across his leg, his hands were bleeding and quivering with pain.

But he had reached the sill, and that was everything.

He pushed up the narrow window, and with much difficulty forced his little fat body through. Then he dropped down on to a shelf, and lowered himself gingerly on to the floor. There was no time to stay to look at his many hurts, he merely regarded the biggest scratch with rueful eyes, and then began to look around for provender. The pantry was remarkably empty—not a sign of cakes, not a bit of jelly, not a remnant of fowl anywhere. He cut a great piece off a loaf, and carefully wrapped some butter in a scrap of newspaper. There was some corned beef on a dish, and he cut off a thick lump and rolled it up with the remains of a loquat tart. These parcels he disposed of down the loose front of his sailor coat, filling up his pockets with sultanas, citron-peel, currants, and such dainties as the store bottles held. And then he prepared to make his painful retreat.

He climbed upon the shelf once more, put his head out of the window, and gave a look of despair at the cactus. And even as he knelt there sounded behind him the sharp click of a turning key.

He looked wildly round, and there was Martha in the doorway, and to his utter horror she was talking to his father, who was in the passage just beyond.

"Row's Embrocation, or arnica," the Captain was saying. "It is probably in this pantry, my good girl, because it is the last place I should expect it to be in. I left it on my bedroom mantelpiece, but somebody has seen fit to meddle with it. Why in the name of all that is mysterious can't you let my things alone?"

"And for what should I be after moving it for?" Martha retorted. "I don't mix the pastry with it to make it lightsome, leastway not ordinarily."

She tossed her head, and the action revealed the small, kneeling, terrified figure at the window.

Now the door was only half open, and her master was standing just beside it outside, so she only had the benefit of the spectacle.

Twice she opened her mouth to speak, but Bunty made such frantic, imploring faces at her that she closed it again, and even began to examine the bottles on the shelf near the door to give the boy an opportunity of retreat.

One minute and he would have been safe—one

minute and he would have been in the thick of the cactus, that had quite lost its terrors.

But the Fates were too strong for him. And all because Martha Tomlinson's shoe was down at the heel. In turning round it twisted a little under her, and, in trying to recover her balance, she put out one hand. And in putting out one hand she knocked over a jug. And the jug communicated its shock to a dish. Which toppled over, and coolly pushed the great basin of milk off the shelf on to the floor. I don't know if ever you have tried to clean a board floor after milk, but I am sure you can imagine it would be a disagreeable task— especially if you had scrubbed it well only that morning. It was hardly to be wondered at, therefore, that Martha, in her profound irritation at the disaster, turned angrily round, and, pointing to the figure now stuck in the window, demanded in an exasperated tone whether the blessed saints could stand that dratted boy any longer, for she couldn't, so there.

The Captain took an angry step into the pantry and gave a roar of command for Bunty to come down.

The boy dropped in an agony of dread and shrinking.

"Always his hands a-pickin' and stealin' and his tongue a-lyin'," said Martha Tomlinson, gazing unkindly at the unhappy child.

Two, three, four, five angry cuts from the riding-whip in the Captain's hands, and Bunty had ducked under his arm and fled howling down the passage and out of the back door.

Away across the paddocks he went, sobbing at every step, but hugely commending himself for bearing all this for someone else's sake.

He could hardly have believed, had anyone told him previously, that he could have done anything so absolutely noble, and the thought comforted him even while the cuts and scratches smarted. He tried to stifle his sobs as he reached the shed, and even stuffed half a handful of currants into his mouth towards that end.

But it was a very tearful, scratched, miserable face that bobbed up the opening near Judy again.

She did not move, though her eyes were half open, and he knelt down and shook her shoulder gently.

" Here's some things, Judy—ain't you goin' to eat them ? "

She shook her head very slightly.

"Have some corned beef, or some currants; there's some peel, too, if you'd rather."

She shook her head again. " Do take them away," she said, with a little moan.

A look of blank disappointment stole over his small, heated face.

"An' I've half killed myself to get them! Well, you *are* a mean girl! " he said.

"Oh, *do* go away," Judy moaned, moving her head restlessly from side to side. " Oh, how my feet ache! no—my head, and my side—oh! I don't know what it is! "

" I got hit here and here," Bunty said, indicating the places, and wiping away tears of keen self-pity with his coat sleeve. "I'm scratched all over with that beastly old cactus."

"Do you suppose there are many miles more?" Judy said, in such a quick way that all the words seemed to run into each other. "I've walked hundreds and hundreds, and haven't got home yet. I suppose it's because the world's round, and I'll be walking in at the school gate again presently."

"Don't be an idjut!" Bunty said gruffly.

"You'll be sure and certain, Marian, never to breathe a word of it; I've trusted you, and if you keep faith I can go home and come back and no one will know. And lend me two shillings, can you? I've not got much left. Bunty, you selfish little pig, you might get me some milk! I've been begging and begging of you for hours, and my head is going to Catherine wheels for want of it."

"Have some corned beef, Judy, dear—oh, Judy, don't be so silly and horrid after I nearly got killed for you," Bunty said, trying with trembling fingers to stuff a piece into her mouth.

The little girl rolled over and began muttering again.

"Seventy-seven miles," she said, "and I walked eleven yesterday, that makes eleven hundred and seventy-seven—and six the day before because my foot had a blister—that's eleven hundred and eighty-three. And if I walk ten miles a day I shall get home in eleven hundred and eighty-three times ten, that's a thousand and—and—oh! what is it? whatever is it? Bunty, you horrid little pig, can't you tell me what it is? My head aches too much to work, and a thousand and something days—that's a year—two years—two years—three years before I get there. Oh, Pip, Meg, three years! oh, Esther! ask him, ask him to let me come home! Three years—years—years!"

The last word was almost shrieked and the child struggled to her feet and tried to walk.

Bunty caught her arms and held her. "Let me go, can't you?" she said hoarsely. "I shall never get there at this rate. Three years, and all those miles!"

She pushed him aside and tried to walk across the loft, but her legs tottered under her and she fell down in a little senseless heap. "Meg—I'll fetch Meg," said the little boy in a trembling, alarmed voice, and he slipped down the opening and hastened up to the house.

CHAPTER 11

The Truant

HE BURST INTO MEG'S BEDROOM like a whirlwind. "She's in the old shed, Meg, and I'm not sure, but I think she's gone mad; and I've had the awfullest beating, and got nearly killed with the cactus for her, and never told anything. She can't eat the corned beef, either, after all. She's run away—and oh, I'm sure she's mad!"

Meg lifted a pale, startled face from the pillows. "Who on earth—what——"

"Judy," he said, and burst into excited sobs. "She's in the shed, and I think she's mad!"

Meg got slowly out of bed, huddled on some clothes, and, even then utterly disbelieving the wild story, went downstairs with him.

In the hall they met their father, who was just going out.

"Are you better?" he said to Meg. "You should have stayed in bed all day; however, perhaps the air will do you more good."

"Yes," she said mechanically.

"I'm going out for the rest of the day; indeed, I don't expect either Esther or myself will be back till to-morrow morning."

"Yes," repeated Meg.

"Don't let the children blow the house up, and take care of yourself—oh! and send Bunty to bed without any tea—he's had enough for one day, I'm sure."

"Yes," said the girl again, only taking in the import of what the last pledged her to when Bunty whispered a fierce "Sneak!" at her elbow.

Then the dogcart rattled up, and the Captain went away, to their unspeakable relief.

"Now what is this mad story?" Meg said, turning to her small brother. "I suppose it's one of your untruths, you bad little boy."

"Come and see," Bunty returned, and he led the way through the paddocks. Half-way down they met Pip and Nell, returning earlier than expected from the fishing expedition. Nellie looked sad, and was walking at a respectful distance behind her brother.

"You might as well take a phonograph with you as Nellie," he said, casting a look of withering scorn on that delinquent. "She talked the whole time, and didn't give me a chance of a bite."

"Judy's home," said Bunty, almost bursting with the importance of his knowledge. "No one's seen her but me; I've nearly got killed with climbing up cactuses and into windows and things, and I've had thrashings from Father and everything, but I never told a word, did I, Meg? I've got her up in the shed here, and I went and got corned beef and everything—just you look at my legs."

He displayed his scars proudly, but Meg hurried

on, and Pip and Nell followed in blank amazement. At the shed they stopped.

"It's a yarn of Bunty's," Pip said contemptuously. "'Tisn't April the first yet, my son."

"Come and see," Bunty returned, swarming up. Pip followed, and gave a low cry; then Meg and Nell, with rather more difficulty, scrambled up, and the scene was complete.

The delirium had passed, and Judy was lying with wide-open eyes gazing in a tired way at the rafters.

She smiled up at them as they gathered round her. "If Mahomet won't come to the mountain," she said, and then coughed for two or three minutes.

"What have you been doing, Ju, old girl?" Pip said, with an odd tremble in his voice. The sight of his favourite sister, thin, hollow-cheeked, exhausted, was too much for his boyish manliness. A moisture came to his eyes.

"How d'you come, Ju?" he said, blinking it away.

And the girl gave her old bright look up at him. "Sure and they keep no pony but shank's at school," she said; "were you afther thinkin' I should charter a balloon?"

She coughed again.

Meg dropped down on her knees and put her arms round her little thin sister.

"Judy," she cried, "oh, Judy, Judy! my dear, my dear!"

Judy laughed for a little time, and called her an old silly, but she soon broke down and sobbed

convulsively. "I'm *so* hungry," she said at last
pitifully.

They all four started up as though they would
fetch the stores of Sydney to satisfy her. Then Meg
sat down again and lifted the rough, curly head on
her lap.

"You go, Pip," she said, "and bring wine and a
glass, and in the meat-safe there's some roast
chicken; I had it for my lunch, and Martha said she
would put the rest there till tea; and be quick,
Pip."

"My word!" said Pip to himself, and he slipped
down and flew across to the house.

"Up*on* my word!" said Martha, meeting him in
the hall five minutes later, a cut-glass decanter
under his arm, a wineglass held in his teeth by the
stem, a dish of cold chicken in his hand, and bread
and butter in a little stack beside the chicken.
"Up*on* my word! And what next, might I ask?"

"Oh, shut up, and hang your grandmother!"
said Pip, brushing past her, and going a circuitous
voyage to the shed lest she should be watching.

He knelt down beside his little sister and fed her
with morsels of chicken and sips of wine, and
stroked her wild hair, and called her old girl fifty
times, and besought her to eat just a little more and
a little more.

And Judy, catching the look in the brown, wet
eyes above her, ate all he offered, though the first
mouthful nearly choked her; she would have eaten
it had it been elephant's hide, seeing she loved this
boy better than anything else in the world, and he
was in such distress. She was the better for it, too,

and sat up and talked quite naturally after a little time.

"You shouldn't have done it, you shouldn't really, you know, old girl; and what the governor will say to you beats me."

"He won't know," she answered quickly. "I'd never forgive whoever told him. I can only stay a week. I've arranged it all beautifully, and I shall live here in this loft; Father never dreams of coming here, so it will be quite safe, and you can all bring me food. And then after a week"—she sighed heavily—"I must go back again."

"Did you really walk all those miles just to see us?" Pip said, and again there was the strange note in his voice.

"I got a lift or two on the way," she said, "but I walked nearly all of it, I've been coming for nearly a week."

"How *could* you do it? Where did you sleep, Judy? What did you eat?" Meg exclaimed, in deep distress.

"I nearly forget," Judy said, closing her eyes again. "I kept asking for food at little cottages, and sometimes they asked me to sleep, and I had three-and-six—that went a long way. I only slept outside two nights, and I had my jacket then."

Meg's face was pale with horror at her sister's adventure. Surely no girl in the wide world but Judy Woolcot would have attempted such a hare-brained project as walking all those miles with three-and-six in her pocket.

"How *could* you?" was all she could find to say.

"I hadn't meant to walk all the way," Judy said,

with a faint smile. "I had seven shillings in a bit of paper in my pocket, as well as the three-and-six, and I knew it would take me a long way in the train. But then I lost it after I had started, and I didn't believe in going back just for that, so, of course, I had to walk."

Meg touched her cheek softly.

"It's no wonder you got so thin," she said.

"Won't the Miss Burtons be raising a hue-and-cry after you?" Pip asked. "It's a wonder they've not written to the pater to say you have ske-daddled."

"Oh! Marian and I made that all safe," Judy said, with a smile of recollective pleasure. "Marian's my chum, you see, and does anything I tell her. And she lives at Katoomba."

"Well?" said Meg, mystified, as her sister paused.

"Well, you see, a lot of the girls had the measles, and so they sent for Marian home, for fear she should get them. And Marian's mother asked for me to go there, too, for a fortnight; and so Miss Burton wrote and asked Father could I? and I wrote and asked couldn't I come home instead for the time?"

"He never told us," Meg said softly.

"No, I s'pose not. Well, he wrote back and said 'no' to me and 'yes' to her. So one day they put us in the train safely, and we were to be met at Katoomba. And the thought jumped into my head as we went along: Why ever shouldn't I come home on the quiet? So I told Marian she could explain to her people I had gone home instead, and that she was to be sure to make it seem all right, so they wouldn't write to Miss Burton. And then the train stopped at Blackheath, and I jumped straight out, and she went on to Katoomba, and I came home. That's all. Only, you see, as I'd lost my money there was nothing left for it but to walk."

Meg smoothed the dusty, tangled confusion of her hair.

"But you can't live out here for the week," she said, in a troubled voice. "You've got a horrid cough with sleeping outside, and I'm sure you're ill. We shall have to tell Father about it. I'll beg him not to send you back, though."

Judy started up, her eyes aflame.

"If you do," she said—"if you do, I will run away this very night, and walk to Melbourne, or Jerusalem, and never see any of you again! How *can* you, Meg! After I've done all this just so he wouldn't know! Oh, how *can* you?"

She was working herself up into a strong state of excitement.

"Why, I should be simply packed back again to-morrow—you know I would, Meg. Shouldn't I now, Pip? And get into a fearful row at school into the bargain. My plan is beautifully simple. After I've had a week's fun here with you I shall just go back—you can all lend me some money for the train. I shall just meet Marian at Katoomba on the 25th; we shall both go back to school together, and no one will be a bit the wiser. My cough's nothing; you know I often do get coughs at home, and they never hurt me. As long as you bring me plenty to eat, and stay with me, I'll be all right."

The rest and food and home faces had done

much already for her; her face looked less pinched, and a little more wholesome colour was creeping slowly into her cheeks.

Meg had an uncomfortable sense of responsibility, and the feeling that she ought to tell someone was strong upon her; but she was overruled by the others in the end.

"You *couldn't* be so mean, Meg," Judy had said warmly, when she had implored to be allowed to tell Esther.

"Such a blab!" Bunty had added.

"Such an awful sneak!" Pip had said.

So Meg held her tongue, but was exceedingly unhappy.

CHAPTER 12

Swish, Swish!

ON THE FOURTH DAY of Judy's residence in the loft, Martha Tomlinson remarked to her fellow-servant and sufferer, Bridget, that she believed them blessed children were in a conspiracy to put her "over the river."

Bridget's digestion was impaired that morning, and she merely remarked that she supposed the dear little things only felt a desire to see her in her proper place.

I should explain to you, perhaps, that "over the river" meant Gladesville, which is Sydney's Colney Hatch.

Many things had led the unhappy Martha to a belief in this conspiracy. For instance, when she went to make Pip's bed as usual one morning all the bedclothes had gone. The white counterpane was spread smoothly over the mattress, but there was absolutely no trace of the blankets, sheets, and pillows. She hunted in every possible and impossible place, questioned the children, and even applied to Esther, but the missing things could not be found.

"There's a man in corduroy trousers hanging

round here every night," Pip said, gloomily regarding his stripped bed. "I shouldn't wonder if he had something to do with it."

Which suggestion was distinctly unkind, seeing the man in corduroy trousers was Martha's most ardent and favoured admirer.

The next day the washing basin in Meg's room went, and after that a chair from the nursery, and a strip of carpet from the top landing, not to mention such small things as a teapot, a spirit-lamp, cups and plates, half a ham, and a whole baking of gingerbread nuts.

The losses preyed upon Martha, for the things seemed to disappear while the children were in bed; and though she suspected them, and watched them continually, she could get no clear proof of their guilt, nor even find any motive for them abstracting such things.

And after the disappearance of each fresh article, Pip used to ask whether the corduroy-trousered gentleman had been to the house the night before. And as it always happened that he had, Martha could do nothing but cast a wrathful glance at the boy and flounce from the room.

One night the little chess-table from the nursery was spirited away.

Pip fell upon Martha's neck the next morning early, as she was sweeping the carpet, and affected to be dissolved in tears.

"'We never prize the violet,'" he said, in broken tones. "Ah! Martha, Martha! we never felt what a treasure we had in you till now, when your days with us are numbered."

"Get along with you," she said, hitting out at him with the broom handle. "And I ain't a-goin' to leave, so don't you think it. You'd have it your own way then too much. No, you don't get shut of Martha Tomlinson just yet, young man."

"But won't he be wanting you, Martha?" he said gently. "His furnishing *must* be nearly finished now. He's not taken a saucepan yet, nor a flat-iron, I know; but there's everything else, Martha; and I don't mind telling you in confidence I'm think-ing of giving you a flat-iron myself as a wedding present, so you needn't wait till he comes for that."

"Get out with you!" said Martha again, thrust-ing the broom-head right into his face, and nearly choking him with dust. "It's a limb of the old gentleman himself you are."

Away in the loft things were getting very com-fortable.

A couple of rugs hung on the walls kept out the draught. Judy's bed, soft and warm, was in a corner; she had a chair to sit in, a table to eat at, even a basin in which to perform her ablutions. And she had company all day, and nearly always all night. Once Meg had stolen away, after fastening her bedroom door, and had shared the bed in the loft; once Nellie had gone, and the other night Pip had taken a couple of blankets and made himself a shakedown among the straw. They used to pay her visits at all hours of the day, creeping up the creak-ing ladder one after the other, whenever they could get away unnoticed.

The governess had, as it happened, a fortnight's

holiday, to nurse a sick mother, so the girls and Bunty had no demands on their time. * Pip used to go to school late and come back early, cajoling notes of excuse, whenever possible, out of Esther. He even played the truant once, and took a caning for it afterwards quite good-humouredly.

Judy still looked pale and tired, and her cough was rather troublesome; but she was fast getting her high spirits back, and was enjoying her adventure immensely.

The only drawback was the cribbed, cabined, and confined space of the loft.

"You will *have* to arrange things so that I can go for a run," she said one morning, in a determined manner. "My legs are growing shorter, I am sure, with not exercising them. I shall have forgotten how to walk by the end of the week."

Pip didn't think it could be done; Meg besought her to run no risks; but Bunty and Nell were eager for it.

"Meg could talk to Father," Bunty said, "and Pip could keep teasing General till Esther would be frightened to leave the room, and then me and Judy would nick down and have a run, and get back before you let them go."

Judy shook her head.

"That would be awfully stale," she said. "If I go, I shall stay down some time. Why shouldn't we have a picnic down at the river?"

"Oh, yes, let's!" Bunty cried, with sparkling eyes.

"I'm sure we could manage it, especially as it's Saturday, and Pip hasn't to go to school," Judy

H   113 continued, thinking it rapidly out. "Two of you could go and get some food. Tell Martha you are all going for a picnic—she'll be glad enough not to have dinner to set—then you go on. Two others can watch if the coast's clear while I get down and across the paddocks, and once we're at the corner of the road we're safe."

It seemed feasible enough, and in a very short time the preparations were all made. Pip was mounting guard at the shed, and had undertaken to get Judy safely away, and Bunty had been stationed on the back veranda to keep *cave* and whistle three times if there was any danger.

He was to wait for a quarter of an hour by the kitchen clock, and then, if all was well, to bring the big billy and a bread loaf, and catch the others up on the road.

It was slow work waiting there, and he stood on one leg, like a meditative fowl, and reviewed the events of the last few exciting days.

He had a depressed feeling at his heart, but why he could hardly tell. Perhaps it was the lie he had told his father, and which was still unconfessed, because the horse was seriously lame, and his courage oozed away every time he thought of that riding-whip.

Perhaps it was the reaction after the great excitement. Or it may have been a rankling sense of injustice at the small glory his brave deeds on Judy's behalf evoked from the others. They did not seem to attach any importance to them, and, indeed, laughed every time he alluded to them or drew public attention to his scars. Two or three of the scratches on his legs were really bad ones, and while he was standing waiting he turned down his stockings and gazed at them with pitying eyes and something like a sob in his throat.

"Nobody cares!" he muttered, and one of his ever-ready tears fell splashing down on one extended bare leg. "Judy likes Pip best, and *he* never climbed the cactus; Meg thinks I tell stories; and Nellie says I'm a greedy pig—nobody cares!"

Another great fat tear gathered and fell.

"Have you taken root there?" a voice asked.

His father, smoking at the open french window, had been watching him, and marvelling at his rare and exceeding quietness.

Bunty started guiltily, and pulled up his stockings.

"I'm not doin' nothin'," he said aggrievedly, after a minute's pause. Bunty always lapsed into evil grammar when agitated. "Nothing at all. I'm goin' to a picnic."

"Ah, indeed!" said the Captain. "You looked as if you were meditating on some fresh mischief, or sorrowing over some old—which was it?"

Bunty turned a little pale, but remarked again he "wasn't doin' nothin'."

The Captain felt in a lazy, teasing mood, and his little fat, dirty son was the only subject near.

"Suppose you come here and confess every bit of mischief you've done this week," he said gravely. "I've the whole morning to spare, and it's time I saw to your morals a little."

115

Bunty approached the arm of the chair indicated, but went whiter than ever.

"Ah, now we're comfortable. Well, there was stealing from the pantry on Tuesday—that's one," he said, encouragingly. "Now then."

"I n—n—never did n—nothin' else," Bunty gasped. He felt certain it was all over with him, and the cricket ball episode was discovered. He even looked nervously round to see if the riding-whip was near. Yes, there was Esther's silver-topped one flung carelessly on a chair. He found time to wish fervently Esther was a tidy woman.

"Nothing at all, Bunty? On your word?" said his father, in an impressive tone.

"I was p—playin' marbles," he said, in a shaking voice. "How c—c—could I have sh—shot anything at y—y—your old horse?"

"Horse?—ah!" said his father. A light broke upon him, and his face grew stern. "What did you throw at Mazeppa to lame him? Answer me at once."

Bunty gave a shuddering glance at the whip.

"N—n—nothin'," he answered—"n—nothin' at all. My c—c—cricket b—ball was up in the st—st—stables. I was only p—p—playin' marbles."

The Captain gave him a little shake.

"Did you lame Mazeppa with the cricket ball?" he said sternly.

"N—n—no I n—never," Bunty whispered, white to the lips. Then semi-repentance came to him, and he added: "It just rolled out of my p—p—pocket, and M—Mazeppa was passing and h—h—hit his l—leg on it."

116

"Speak the truth, or I'll thrash you within an inch of your life," the Captain said, standing up, and seizing Esther's whip. "Now then, sir—was it you lamed Mazeppa?"

"Yes," said Bunty, bursting into a roar of crying, and madly dodging the whip.

Then, as the strokes descended on his unhappy shoulders, he filled the air with his familiar wail of "'Twasn't me, 'twasn't my fault!"

"You contemptible young cur!" said his father, pausing a moment when his arm ached with wielding the whip. "I'll thrash this mean spirit of lying and cowardice out of you, or kill you in the attempt." Swish, swish. "What sort of a man do you think you'll make?" Swish, swish. "Telling lies just to save your miserable skin!" Swish, swish, swish, swish.

"You've killed me—oh, you've killed me! I know you have!" yelled the wretched child, squirming all over the floor. "'Twasn't me, 'twasn't my fault—hit the others some."

Swish, swish, swish. "Do you think the others would lie so contemptibly? Philip never lied to me. Judy would cut her tongue out first." Swish, swish, swish. "Going to a picnic, are you? You can picnic in your room till to-morrow's breakfast." Swish, swish, swish. "Pah—get away with you!"

Human endurance could go no further. The final swish had been actual agony to his smarting, quivering shoulders and back. He thought of the others, happy and heedless, out in the sunshine, trudging merrily off to the river, without a thought of what he was bearing, and his very heart seemed to burst in the hugeness of its bitterness and despair. "Judy's home!" he said, in a choking, passionate voice. "She lives in the old shed in the cow paddock. Boo, hoo, hoo! They're keepin' it secret from you. Boo, hoo. She's gone to the picnic, and she's run away from school."

CHAPTER 13

Uninvited Guests

THE CAPTAIN WAS WALKING slowly across the paddocks with the cabbage-tree hat he kept for the garden pushed back from his brow. He was rather heated after his tussle with his second son, and there was a thoughtful light in his eyes. He did not believe the truth of Bunty's final remark, but still he considered there was sufficient probability in it to make a visit to the shed not altogether superfluous.

Not that he expected, in any case, to find his errant daughter there, for had not Bunty said there was a picnic down at the river? But he thought there might be some trace or other.

The door of the shed swung back on its crazy hinges, and the sunlight streamed in and made a bar of glorified dust across the place.

There was no sign of habitation here, unless a hair ribbon of Meg's and some orange peel might be considered as such.

He saw the shaky, home-made ladder, resting against the hole in the ceiling, and though he had generally more respect for his neck than his children had for theirs, he ventured his safety upon

119

it. It creaked ominously as he reached the top step and crawled through into the loft.

There were a ham-bone, a box of dominoes, and a burst pillow this side of the partition, nothing else, so he walked across and looked over.

"Very cosy," he murmured, "I shouldn't mind camping here myself for a little time," and it even came into his head to do so, and be there as a "surprise party" when Judy returned. But he dismissed the idea as hardly compatible with dignity. He remembered hearing rumours of missing furniture in the house, and almost a smile came into his eyes as he saw the little old table with the spirit-lamp and teapot thereon, the bed-clothing and washing-basin. But a stern look succeeded it. Were seventy-seven miles not sufficient obstacle to Judy's mischievous plans? How did she dare thus to defy him, a child of thirteen and he her father? His lips compressed ominously, and he went down again and strode heavily back to the house.

"Esther!" he called, in a vibrating voice at the foot of the stairs.

And "Coming, dear—half a minute," floated down in response.

Half a minute passed ten times, and then she came, the beautiful young mother with her laughing-faced wee son in her arms. Her eyes looked so tender, and soft, and loving that he turned away impatiently; he knew quite well how it would be; she would beg and entreat him to forgive his little daughter when she heard, and when she looked as bright and beautiful as she did just now he could refuse her nothing.

He stood in profound meditation for a minute or two.

"What is it you want, John?" she said. "Oh! and what do you think? I have just found another tooth, a double one—come and look."

He came, half unwillingly, and stuck his little finger into his infant son's mouth.

Esther guided it till it felt a tiny, hard substance. "The third," she said proudly; "aren't you pleased?"

"Hum!" he said. Then he meditated a little longer, and after a minute or two rubbed his hands as if he was quite pleased with himself.

"Put on your hat, Esther, and the General's," he said, patting that young gentleman's head affectionately. "Let us go down to the river for a stroll; the children are down there picnicking, so we can be sure of some tea."

"Why, yes, that will be very nice," she said, "won't it, Bababsie, won't it, sweet son?"

She called to Martha, who was dusting the drawing-room in a cheerfully blind way peculiarly hers.

"The General's hat, please, Martha, the white sun-hat with strings; it's on my bed, I think, or a chair or somewhere—oh! and bring down my large one with the poppies in, as well, please."

Martha departed, and, after a little search, returned with the headgear.

And Esther tied the white sun-hat over her own curly, crinkly hair, and made the General crow with laughing from his seat on the hall table. And then she popped it on the Captain's head, and put the cabbage-tree on her son's, and occupied several minutes thus in pretty play.

Finally they were ready, and moved down the hall.

"Master Bunty is locked in his room; on no account open the door, Martha," was the Captain's last command.

"Oh, Jack!" Esther said reproachfully.

"Oblige me by not interfering," he said; "allow me a little liberty with my own children, Esther. He is an untruthful little vagabond; I am ashamed to own him for my son."

And Esther, reflecting on the many shiftinesses of her stepson, was able to console herself with the hope that it would do him good.

They went a short cut through the bush to avoid the public road, and the blue, sun-kissed, laughing river stretched before them.

"There they are," Esther cried, "in the old place, as usual; look at the fire, little sweet son; see the smoke, boy bonny—four—five of them. Why, who have they got with them?" she said in surprise, as they drew nearer the group on the grass.

Before they were close enough to recognize faces the circle suddenly seemed to break up and fall apart.

One of its members turned sharply round and fled away across the grass, plunging into the thick bracken and bush, and disappearing from sight in less time than it takes to tell.

"Whoever had you with you?" Esther said when they reached the children.

There was a half-second's silence, then Pip threw some sticks on the fire and said coolly:

"Only a friend of Meg's, a frightened kind of kid who has quite a dread of the pater. I believe she imagines soldiers go round with their swords sharpened, ready for use."

He laughed lightly. Nell joined in in a little hysterical way, and Baby began to cry.

Meg, white as death, picked her up and hurriedly began telling her the story of the three bears for comfort.

Esther looked a little puzzled, but, of course, never dreamt of connecting the flying figure with Judy.

And the Captain seemed delightfully blind and unsuspicious. He lay down on the grass and let the General swarm all over him; he made jokes with Esther; he told several stories of his young days, and never even seemed to remark that his audience seemed inattentive and constrained.

"Haven't you made some tea?" Esther said at last. "We love billy tea, and thought you would be sure to have some?"

"Bunty hasn't come, he was to have brought the billy," Pip said, half sulkily. He had suspicions that there was something behind this great affability of his father, and he objected to being played with.

"Ah," the Captain said gravely, "that is unfortunate. When I came away Bunty did not seem very well, and was thinking of spending the rest of the day in his bedroom."

Pip made up the fire in a dogged way, and Meg

flashed a frightened glance at her father, who smiled affectionately back at her.

After an hour of this strained intercourse the Captain proposed a return home.

"It is growing chill," he said. "I should be grieved for the General's new-born tooth to start its life by aching—let's go home and make shift with teapot tea."

So they gathered up the untouched baskets and made themselves into a procession.

The Captain insisted on Pip and Meg walking with him, and he sent Baby and Nell on in front, one on either side of Esther, who was alternately leading and carrying the General.

This arrangement being, as indeed Pip shrewdly suspected, to prevent the possibility of any intercourse or formation of new plans.

And when they got home he invited them all to come into his smoking-room, a little slit of a place off the dining-room.

Esther took the General upstairs, but the others followed him in silence.

"Sit down, Pip, my boy," he said genially. "Come, Meg, make yourself at home, take a seat in that armchair. Nell and Baby can occupy the lounge."

They all sat down helplessly where he told them, and watched his face anxiously.

He selected a pipe from the row over the mantelpiece, fitted a new mouthpiece to it, and carefully filled it.

"As you are all in possession of my room," he said in an urbane voice, "I can hardly smoke with any comfort here, I am afraid. I will come and talk to you again later on. I am going to have a pipe first in the old loft in the cow paddock. Keep out of mischief till I come back."

He struck a match, lighted his tobacco, and, without a glance at the silent children, left the room, locking the door behind him.

Once more he crossed the paddocks, and once more pushed open the creaking door. The orange peel lay just where he had seen it before, only it was a little drier and more dead-looking. The hair ribbon was in exactly the same knot. The ladder creaked in just the same place, and again threatened to break his neck when he reached the top. The dominoes were there still, the ham-bone and the pillow occupied the same places; the only difference being the former had a black covering of ants now, and a wind had been playing with the pillow, and had carried the feathers in all directions.

He crossed the floor, not softly, but just with his usual measured military step. Nothing moved. He reached the partition and looked over.

Judy lay across the improvised bed, sleeping a sleep of utter exhaustion after her rapid flight from the river. She had a frock of Meg's on, that made her look surprisingly long and thin; he was astonished to think she had grown so much.

"There will be no end to my trouble with her as she grows older," he said, half aloud, feeling extremely sorry for himself for being her father. Then a great anger and irritation rose within him as he watched her sleeping so quietly there. Was she always to be a disturber of his peace? Was she always to thwart him like this?

" Judy," he said in a loud voice.

The closed eyelids sprang open, the mist of sleep and forgetfulness cleared from the dark eyes, and she sprang up, a look of absolute horror on her face.

"What are you doing here, may I ask?" he said, very coldly.

The scarlet colour flooded her cheeks, her very brow, and then dropped down again, leaving her white to the lips, but she made no answer.

"You have run away from school, I suppose?" he continued, in the same unemotional voice. "Have you anything to say?"

Judy did not speak or move, she only watched his face with parted lips.

" Have you anything to say for yourself, Helen?" he repeated.

"No, Father," she said.

Her face had a worn, strained look that might have touched him at another time, but he was too angry to notice.

" No excuse or reason at all?"

"No, Father."

He moved toward the opening. "A train goes in an hour and a half, you will come straight back with me this moment," he said, in an even voice. "I shall take precautions to have you watched at school since you cannot be trusted. You will not return home for the Christmas holidays, and probably not for those of the following June."

It was as bad as a sentence of death. The room

swam before the girl's eyes, there was a singing and rushing in her ears.

"Come at once," the Captain said. Judy gave a little caught breath; it tickled her throat and she began to cough.

Such terrible coughing, a paroxysm that shook her thin frame and made her gasp for breath. It lasted two or three minutes, though she put her handkerchief to her mouth to try to stop it.

She was very pale when it ceased, and he noticed the hollows in her cheeks for the first time.

"You had better come to the house first," he said, less harshly, "and see if Esther has any cough stuff."

Then in his turn he caught his breath and grew pale under his bronze.

For the handkerchief that the child had taken from her lips had scarlet, horrible spots staining its whiteness.

CHAPTER 14

The Squatter's Invitation

SO AFTER ALL THERE WAS NO DOGCART for Judy, no mountain train, no ignominious return to the midst of her schoolfellows, no vista of weary months unmarked by holidays.

But instead, a warm, soft bed, and delicate food, and loving voices and ceaseless attention. For the violent exertion, the scanty food, and the two nights in the open air had brought the girl to indeed a perilous pass. One lung was badly inflamed, the doctor said; it was a mystery to him, he kept telling them, how she had kept up so long; an ordinary girl would have given in and taken to her bed long ago. But then he was not acquainted with the indomitable spirit and pluck that were Judy's characteristics.

"Didn't you have any pain?" he asked, quite taken aback to find such spirits and so serious a condition together.

"H'm, in my side sometimes," she answered carelessly. "How long will it be before I can get up, Doctor?"

She used to ask the latter question of him every morning, though, if the truth were known, she felt

128

secretly more than a little diffident at the idea of standing up again.

There was a languor and weariness in her limbs that made her doubtful if she could run about very much, and slower modes of progressing she despised. Besides this, there was a gnawing pain under her arms, and the cough was agony while it lasted.

Still, she was not ill enough to lose interest in all that was going on, and used to insist upon the others telling her everything that happened outside—who made the biggest score at cricket, what flowers were out in her own straggling patch of garden, how many eggs the fowls laid a day, how the guinea-pigs and canaries were progressing, and what was the very latest thing in clothes or boots the new retriever puppy had devoured.

And Bunty used to bring in the white mice and the blind French guinea-pig, and let them run loose over the counterpane; and Pip did most of his carpentering on a little table near, so she could see each fresh stage and suggest improvements as he went along.

Meg, who had almost severed her connection with Aldith, devoted herself to her sister, and waited on her hand and foot; she made her all kinds of little presents—a boot-bag, with compartments; a brush-and-comb bag, with the monogram " J.W.," worked in pink silk; a little work-basket, with needle-book, pin-cushion, and all complete. Judy feared she should be compelled to betake herself to tidy habits on her recovery.

Her pleasure in the little gifts started a spirit of competition among the others.

For one whole day Pip was invisible, but in the evening he turned up, and walked to the bedside with a proud face. He had constructed a little set of drawers, three of which actually opened under skilful coaxing.

"It's not for doll-clothes," he said, after she had exhausted all the expressions of gratitude in common use, "because I know you hate them, but you can keep all your little things in them, you see—hair strings, and thimbles, and things."

There was a sound of dragging outside the door and presently Bunty came in backward, lugging a great, strange thing.

It seemed to be five or six heavy pieces of board nailed together haphazard.

"It's a chair," he explained, wiping the perspiration from his forehead. "Oh! I'm going to put some canvas across it, of course, so you won't fall through; but I thought I'd show it you first."

Judy's eyes smiled, but she thanked him warmly.

"I wasn't goin' to make any stupid thing, like Pip did," the small youth continued, looking deprecatingly at the little drawers. "This is really useful, you see; when you get up you can sit on it, Judy, by the fire and read or sew or something. You like it better'n Pip's, don't you?"

Judy temporized skilfully, and averted offence to either by asking them to put the presents with all the others near the head of the bed.

"What a lot of things you'll have to take back to school, Ju," Nell said, as she added her contribution in the shape of a pair of crochet cuffs and a doll's wool jacket.

But Judy only flashed her a reproachful glance, and turned her face to the wall for the rest of the evening.

That was what had been hanging over her so heavily all this long fortnight in bed—the thought of school in the future.

" What's going to happen to me when I get better, Esther? " she asked next morning, in a depressed way, when her stepmother came to see her. " Is he saving up a lot of beatings for me? And shall I have to go back the first week? "

Esther reassured her.

" You won't go back this quarter at all, very likely not next either, Judy dear. He says you shall go away with some of the others for a change till you get strong; and, between you and me, I think it's very unlikely you will go back ever again."

With this dread removed, Judy mended more rapidly, surprising even the doctor with her powers of recuperation.

In three weeks she was about the house again, thin and great-eyed, but full of nonsense and even mischief once more. The doctor's visits ceased; he said she had made a good recovery so far, but should have change of surroundings, and be taken a long way from sea air.

" Let her run wild for some months, Woolcot," he said at his last visit; " it will take time to quite shake off all this and get her strength and flesh back again."

" Certainly, certainly; she shall go at once," the Captain said.

He could not forget the shock he had received in

the old loft five or six weeks ago, and would have agreed if he had been bidden to take her for a sojourn in the Sahara.

The doctor had told him the mischief done to her lungs was serious.

"I won't say she will ultimately die of consumption," he had said, "but there is always a danger of that vile disease in these nasty cases. And little Miss Judy is such a wild, unquiet subject; she seems to be always in a perfect fever of living, and to possess a capacity for joy and unhappiness quite unknown to slower natures. Take care of her, Woolcot, and she'll make a fine woman some day—ay, a grand woman."

The Captain smoked four big cigars in the solitude of his study before he could decide how he could best "take care of her."

At first he thought he would send her with Meg and the governess to the mountains for a time, but then there was the difficulty about lessons for the other three. He might send them to school, or engage a governess certainly, but then again there was expense to be considered.

It was out of the question for the girls to go alone, for Meg had shown herself nothing but a silly little goose, in spite of her sixteen years; and Judy needed attention. Then he remembered Esther, too, was looking unwell; the nursing and the General together had been too much for her, and she looked quite a shadow of her bright self. He knew he really ought to send her, too, and the child, of course.

And again the expense.

And again the other children.

He remembered the Christmas holidays were not very far away; what would become of the house with Pip and Bunty and the two youngest girls running wild, and no one in authority? He sighed heavily, and knocked the ash from his fourth cigar upon the carpet.

Then the postman came along the drive and past the window. He looked up with a broad smile, and touched his helmet in a pleased kind of way. It almost seemed as if he knew that in one of the letters he held the solution of the problem that was making the Captain's brow all criss-crossed with frowning lines.

A fifth cigar was being extracted from the case, a wrinkle was deepening just over the left eyebrow, a twinge of something very like gout was calling forth a word or two of "foreign language," when Esther came in with a smile on her lips and an open letter in her hands.

"From Mother," she said. "Yarrahappini's a wilderness, it seems, and she wants me to go up, and take the General with me, for a few weeks."

"Ah!" he said.

It would certainly solve one of the difficulties. The place was very far away certainly, but then it was Esther's old home, and she had not seen it since her marriage. She would grow strong again there very quickly.

"Oh, and Judy, too."

"Ah-h-h!" he said.

Two of the lines smoothed themselves carefully from his brow.

133

"And Meg, because I mentioned she was looking pale."

The Captain placed the cigar back in the case. He forgot there was such a thing as gout.

"The invitation could not have been more opportune," he said. "Accept by all means; nothing could have been better; and it is an exceedingly healthy climate. The other children can——"

"Oh, Father expressly stipulates for Pip as well, because he is a scamp."

"Upon my word, Esther, your parents have a large enough fund of philanthropy. Anyone else included in the invitation?"

"Only Nell and Bunty and Baby. Oh, and Mother says if you can run up at any time for a few days' shooting you know without her telling you how pleased she will be to see you."

"The hospitality of squatters is world-famed, but this breaks all previous records, Esther." The Captain got up and stretched himself with the air of a man released from a nightmare. "Accept by all means—every one of you. On their own heads be the results; but I'm afraid Yarrahappini will be a sadder and wiser place before the month is over."

But just how much sadder or how much wiser he never dreamed.

CHAPTER 15

Three Hundred Miles in the Train

THEY FILLED A WHOLE COMPARTMENT—
at least there was one seat vacant, but people seemed
shy of taking it after a rapid survey of them all.

The whole seven of them, and only Esther as
bodyguard—Esther in a pink blouse and sailor hat,
with a face as bright and mischievous as Pip's
own.

The Captain had come to see them off, with Pat
to look after the luggage. He had bought the
tickets—two whole ones for Esther and Meg, and
four halves for the others. Baby was not provided
with even a half, much to her private indignation
—it was an insult to her four years and a half, she
considered, to go free like the General.

But the cost of those scraps of pasteboard had
made the Captain look unhappy: he only received
eighteenpence change out of the ten pounds he had
tendered; for Yarrahappini was on the borders of
the Never-Never Land.

He spent the eighteenpence on illustrated papers
—*Scraps, Ally Sloper's Half-Holiday, Comic Cuts,
Funny Folks,* and the like, evidently having no very
exalted opinion of the literary tastes of his family;

and he provided Esther with a yellow-back—on which was depicted a lady in a green dress fainting in the arms of a gentleman attired in purple, and Meg with Mark Twain's *Jumping Frog*, because he had noticed a certain air of melancholy in her eyes lately.

Then bells clanged and a whistle shrieked, porters flew wildly about, and farewells were said, sadly or gaily as the case might be.

There was a woman crying in a hopeless little way on the platform, and a girl with sorrowful, loving eyes leaning out of a second-class window towards her; there was a brown-faced squatter, in a tweed cap and slippers, to whom the three-hundred-mile journey was little more of an event than dining; and there was the young man going selecting, and thinking England was little farther, seeing his wife and child were waving a year's good-bye from the platform. There were sportsmen going two hundred miles after quail and wallaby; and cars full of ladies returning to the wilds after their yearly or half-yearly tilt with society and fashion in Sydney; and there were the eight we are interested in, clustering around the door and two windows, smiling and waving cheerful good-byes to the Captain.

He did not look at all cast down as the train steamed fussily away—indeed, he walked down the platform with almost a jaunty air as if the prospect of two months' bachelordom was not without its redeeming points.

It was half-past six in the afternoon when they started, and they would reach Curlewis, which was the nearest railway station to Yarrahappini, about five the next morning. The expense of sleeping-berths had been out of the question with so many of them; but in the rack with the bags were several rolls of rugs and two or three air-pillows against the weary hours. The idea of so many hours in the train had been delightful to all the young ones; none of them but Judy had been a greater distance than forty or fifty miles before, and it seemed perfectly fascinating to think of rushing on and on through the blackness as well as the daylight.

But long before ten o'clock a change came o'er the spirit of their dreams. Nell and Baby had had a quarrel over the puffing out of the air-cushions, and were too tired and cross to make it up again; Pip had hit Bunty over the head for no ostensible reason, and received two kicks in return; Judy's head ached, and the noise was not calculated to cure it; Meg had grown weary of staring out into the moving darkness, and wondering whether Alan would notice she was never on the river-boat now; and the poor little General was filling the hot air with ex-postulations, in the shape of loud roars, at the irregularities of the treatment he was undergoing.

Esther had taken his day clothes off, and made a picture of him in a cream flannel nightgown and a pink wool jacket. And for half an hour he had submitted good-temperedly to being handed about and tickled and half-smothered with kisses. He had even permitted Nell to bite his little pink toes severally, and say a surprising amount of nonsense about little pigs that went to market and did similarly absurd things.

He had hardly remonstrated when there had been

a dispute about the possession of his person, and Bunty had clung to his head and body while Nell pulled vigorously at his legs.

But after a time, when Esther made him a little bed on one of the seats and tried to lay him down upon it, a sense of his grievances came over him.

He had a swinging cot at home, with little gold bars at the foot to blink at—he could not see why he should be mulcted of it, and made to put up with a rug three times doubled. He was accustomed, too, to a shaded light, a quiet room, and a warning H'sh! h'sh! whenever people forgot themselves sufficiently to make the slightest noise.

Here the great yellow light flared all the time, and every one of the noisy creatures at whose hands he endured so much was within a few feet of him.

So he lifted up his voice and wept. And when he found weeping did not produce his gold-barred cot, and the little dangling tassels on the mosquito nets, he raised his voice two notes, and when even then Esther only went on patting his shoulder in a soothing way he burst into roars absolutely deafening.

Nellie dangled all her long curls in his face to engage his attention, but he clutched them viciously and pulled till the tears came into her eyes. Esther and Meg sang lullabies till their tongues ached, Judy tried walking him up and down the narrow space, but he stiffened himself in her arms, and she was not strong enough to hold him. Finally he dropped off into an exhausted sleep, drawing deep, sobbing breaths and little hiccoughs of sorrow.

Then Bunty was discovered asleep on the floor

with his head under a seat, and had to be lifted into an easier position; and Baby, bolt upright in a corner, was nodding like a little pink-and-white daisy the sun has been too much for.

One by one the long hours dragged away; farther and farther through the silent, sleeping country flew the red-eyed train, swerving round zigzag curves, slackening up steeper places, flashing across the endless stretching plains.

The blackness grew grey and paler grey, and miles and miles of monotonous gum saplings lay between the train and sky. Up burst the sun, and the world grew soft and rosy like a baby waked from sleep. Then the grey gathered again, the pink, quivering lights faded out, and the rain came down —torrents of it, beating against the shaking window-glass, whirled wildly ahead by a rough morning wind, flying down from the mountains. Such a crushed, dull-eyed, subdued-looking eight they were as they tumbled out on the Curlewis platform when five o'clock came. Judy coughed at the wet, early air, and was hurried into the waiting-room and wrapped in a rug.

Then the train tossed out their trunks and portmanteaux and rushed on again, leaving them desolate and miserable, looking after it, for it seemed no one had come to meet them.

The sound of wet wheels slushing through puddles, the crack of a whip, the even falling of horses' feet, and they were all outside again, looking beyond the white railway palings to the road.

There were a big, covered waggonette driven by a wide yellow oil-skin with a man somewhere in its

139

interior, and a high buggy, from which an immensely tall man was climbing.

"Father!"

Esther rushed out into the rain. She put her arms round the dripping mackintosh and clung fast to it for a minute or two. Perhaps that is what made her cheeks and eyes so wet and shining.

"Little girl—little Esther child!" he said, and almost lifted her off the ground as he kissed her, tall though Meg considered her.

Then he hurried them all off into the buggies, five in one and three in the other. There was a twenty-five-mile drive before them yet.

"When did you have anything to eat last?" he asked; the depressed looks of the children were making him quite unhappy. "Mother has sent you biscuits and sandwiches, but we can't get coffee or anything hot till we get home."

Nine o'clock, Esther told him, at Newcastle, but it was so boiling hot they had had to leave most of it in their cups and scramble into the train again. The horses were whipped up, and flew over the muddy roads at a pace that Pip, despite his weariness, could not but admire.

But it was a very damp, miserable drive, and the General wept with hardly a break from start to finish, greatly to Esther's vexation, for it was his first introduction to his grandfather.

At last, when everyone was beginning to feel the very end of patience had come, a high white gate broke the monotony of dripping wet fences.

"Home!" Esther said joyfully. She jumped the General up and down on her knee.

"Little Boy Blue, Mum fell off that gate when she was three," said she, looking at it affectionately as Pip swung it open.

Splash through the rain again; the wheels went softly now, for the way was covered with wet fallen leaves.

"Oh, where *is* the house?" Bunty said, peeping through Pip's arm on the box seat, and seeing still nothing but an endless vista of gum trees. "I thought you said we were there, Esther."

"Oh, the front door is not quite so near the gate as at Misrule," she said. And indeed it was not.

It was fifteen minutes before they even saw the chimneys, then there was another gate to be opened.

A gravel drive now, trimly kept, high box round the flower-beds, a wilderness of rose bushes that pleased Meg's eye, two chip tennis-courts under water.

Then the house.

The veranda was all they noticed; such a wide one it was, as wide as an ordinary room, and there were lounges and chairs and tables scattered about, hammocks swung from the corners, and a green thick creeper with rain-blown wistaria for an outer wall.

"O—o—oh," said Pip; "o—oh! I *am* stiff—o—oh, I say, what are you doing?"

For Esther had deposited her infant son on his knee, and leapt out of the waggonette and up the veranda steps.

There was a tiny old lady there, with a great housekeeping apron on. Esther gathered her right

141

up in her arms, and they kissed and clung to each other till they were both crying.

"My little girl!" sobbed the little old lady, stroking, with eager hands, Esther's wet hair and wetter cheeks.

And Bunty, who had followed close behind, looked from the tall figure of his stepmother to the very small one of her mother and laughed.

Esther darted back to the buggy, took the General from Pip, and, springing up the steps again, placed him in her mother's arms.

"Isn't he a fat 'un!" Bunty said, sharing in her pride; "just you look at his legs."

The old lady sat down for one minute in the wettest chair she could find, and cuddled him close up to her.

But he doubled his little cold fists, fought himself free, and yelled for Esther.

Mr. Hassal had emptied the buggies by now, and came up the steps himself.

"Aren't you going to give them some breakfast, little mother?" he said, and the old lady nearly dropped her grandson in her distress.

"Dear, dear!" she said. "Well, well! Just to think of it! But it makes one forget."

In ten minutes they were all in dry things, sitting in the warm dining-room and making prodigious breakfasts.

"*Wasn't* I hungry!" Bunty said. His mouth was full of toast, and he was slicing the top off his fourth egg and keeping an eye on a dish that held honey in one compartment and clotted cream in another.

"The dear old plates!" Esther picked hers up

after she had emptied it and looked lovingly at the blue roses depicted upon it. "And to think the last time I ate off one I——"

"Was a little bride with the veil pushed back from your face," the old lady said, "and everyone watching you cut the cake. Only two have been broken since—oh yes, Hannah, the girl who came after Emily, chipped off the handle of the sugar-basin and broke a bit out of the slop-bowl."

"Where did Father stand?" Meg asked. She was peopling the room with wedding guests; the ham and the chops, the toast and eggs and dishes of fruit, had turned to a great white towered cake with silver leaves.

"Just up there where Pip is sitting," Mrs. Hassal said, "and he was helping Esther with the cake, because she was cutting it with his sword. Such a hole you made in the table-cloth, Esther, my very best damask one with the convolvulus leaves, but, of course, I've darned it—dear, dear!"

Baby had upset her coffee all over herself and her plate and Bunty, who was next door.

She burst into tears of weariness and nervousness at the new people, and slipped off her chair under the table. Meg picked her up.

"May I put her to bed?" she said; "she is about worn out."

"Me, too," Nellie said, laying down her half-eaten scone and pushing back her chair. "Oh, I *am* so tired!"

"So'm I." Bunty finished up everything on his plate in choking haste and stood up. "And that horrid coffee's running into my boots."

So just as the sun began to smile and chase away the sky's heavy tears, they all went to bed again to make up for the broken night, and it was six o'clock and tea-time before any of them opened their eyes again.

CHAPTER 16

Yarrahappini

YARRAHAPPINI IN THE SUNSHINE, the kind of sunshine that pushes the thermometer's silver thread up to 100°!

Right away in the distance on three sides was a blue hill line and blue soft trees.

And up near the house the trees were green and beautiful, and the flowers a blaze of colour.

But all the stretching plain between was brown. Brown burnt grass with occasional patches of dull green, criss-crossed here and there with fences, that ran up the little hills that in places broke the plain's straight line, and disappeared in the dips where rank grass and bracken flourished. The head station consisted of quite a little community of cottages on the top of a hill. Years ago, when Esther was no bigger than her own little General, there had been only a rough, red weather-board place on the hill-top, and a bark hut or two for outhouses.

And Mr. Hassal had been in the saddle from morning to night, and worked harder than any two of his own stockmen, and Mrs. Hassal had laid aside her girlish accomplishments, her fancy work, her

K

guitar, her water-colours, and had scrubbed and cooked and washed as many a settler's wife has done before, until the anxiously watched wool market had brought them better days.

Then a big stone cottage reared itself slowly right in front of the little old place with its bottle-bordered garden plot, where nothing more aristocratic than pig's face and scarlet geranium had ever grown. A beautiful cottage it was, with its plenitude of lofty rooms, its many windows, and its deep veranda. The little red home was kitchen and bedrooms for the two women servants now, and was joined to the big place by a covered way.

A hundred yards away there was a two-roomed cottage that was occupied by the son of an English baronet, who, for the consideration of seventy pounds a year and rations, kept the Yarrahappini business books and gave out the stores.

Farther still, two bark humpies stood, back to back. Tettawonga, a bent old black fellow, lived in one, and did little else than smoke and give his opinion on the weather every morning.

Twenty years ago he had helped to make a steady foundation for the red cottage that had arrived ready built on a bullock-dray.

Fifteen years ago he had killed with his tomahawk one of two bushrangers who were trying to stick up Yarrahappini in the absence of his master, and he had carried little trembling Mrs. Hassal and tiny Esther to a place of safety, and gone back and dealt the other one a blow on the head that stunned him till assistance came.

146

So, of course, he had earned his right to the cottage and the daily rations and the pipe that never stirred from his lips.

Two of the station hands lived in the other cottage when they were not out in distant parts of the run.

Close to the house was a long weather-board building with a heavy, padlocked door.

"Oh, let's go in," Nell said, attracted by the size of the padlock; "it looks like a treasure-house in a book—mayn't we go in, please, little grandma?"

They were exploring all the buildings—the six children in a body, Mrs. Hassal, whom they all called "little grandma," much to her pleasure, and Esther with the boy.

"You must go and ask Mr. Gillet," the old lady said; "he keeps the keys of the stores. See, over in that cottage near the tank, and speak nicely, children, please."

"Such a gentleman," she said in a low tone to Esther, "so clever, so polished, if only he did not drink so."

Meg and Judy went, with Baby hurrying after them as fast as her short legs would allow.

"Come in," a voice said, when they knocked. Meg hesitated nervously, and a man opened the door. Such a great, gaunt man, with restless, unhappy eyes, a brown, wide brow, and neatly trimmed beard.

Judy stated that Mrs. Hassal had sent them for the keys, if he had no objection.

He asked them to come in and sit down while he looked for them.

147

Meg was surprised at the room, as her blue eyes plainly showed, for she had only heard him spoken of as the store-keeper. There were bookshelves, on which she saw Shakespeare and Browning and Shelley and Rossetti and Tennyson, William Morris, and many others she had never seen before. There were neatly framed photographs and engravings of English and Continental scenery on the walls. There was a little chased silver vase on a bracket, and some of the flowers from the passion vines in it. The table with the remains of breakfast on it was as nice on a small scale as the one she had just left in the big cottage.

He came back from the inner room with the keys. "I was afraid I had mislaid them," he said; "the middle one opens the padlock, Miss Woolcot; the brass fat one is for the two bins, and the long steel one for the cupboard."

"Thank you so much. I'm afraid we disturbed you in the middle of your breakfast," Meg said, standing up and blushing because she thought he had noticed her surprise at the bookshelves.

He disclaimed the trouble, and held the door open for them with a bow that had something courtly in it, at least so Meg thought, puzzling how it came to be associated with salt beef by the hundredweight and bins of flour. He watched them go over the grass—at least he watched Meg in her cool, summer muslin and pale-blue belt, Meg in her shady chip hat, with the shining fluffy plait hanging to her waist.

Judy's long black legs and crumpled cambric had no element of the picturesque in them.

148

Mrs. Hassal unfastened the padlock of the store-room.   Such a chorus of "ohs!" and "ahs!" there was from the children!

Baby had never seen so much sugar together in her life before; she looked as if she would have liked to have been let loose in the great bin for an hour or two.

And the currants!   There was a big wooden box brim full—about forty pounds, Mrs. Hassal thought when questioned.

Bunty whipped up a handful and pocketed them when everyone was looking at the mountain of candles.

"Home-made! my *dear*, why, yes, of course," the old lady said.   "Why, I wouldn't dream of using a bought candle, any more than I would use bought soap."

She showed them the great bars of yellow, clean-smelling stuff, with finer, paler-coloured for toilet purposes.

Hams and sides of bacon hung thickly from the rafters.   "Those are mutton hams," she said, point-ing to one division.   "I keep those for the stock-men."

Pip wanted to know if the stores were meant to serve them all their lives, there seemed enough of them: he was astonished to hear that every six months they were replenished.

"Twenty to thirty men, counting the boundary riders and stockmen at different parts of the place, and double that number at shearing or drafting times, not to mention daily sundowners—it's like feeding an army, my dears," she said; "and then,

you see, I had to make preparations for all of you
—Bunty especially."

Her little grey eyes twinkled merrily as she looked
at that small youth.

"You can have them back," Bunty said, half
sulkily. He produced half a dozen currants
from his pocket. "I shouldn't think you'd mind,
with such a lot; we only have a bottleful at
home."

On which the old lady patted his head, un-
locked a tin, and filled his hands with figs and
dates.

"And have you to cook every day for all those
men?" Meg said, wondering what oven could be
found large enough.

"Dear, no!" the old lady answered. "Dear, dear,
no; each man does everything for himself in his own
hut; they don't even get bread, only rations of flour
to make damper for themselves. Then we give them
a fixed quantity of meat, tea, sugar, tobacco, candles,
soap, and one or two other things."

"Where do you keep the wool and things?" said
Pip, who had a soul above home-made soap and
metal dips for candles; "I can't see any shed or
anything."

Mrs. Hassal told him they were a mile away,
down by the creek, where the sheep were washed
and sheared at the proper season. But the heat was
too much to make even Pip want to go just
then, so they attached themselves to Mr. Hassal,
leaving little grandma with Esther, the General,
and Baby, and went over to the brick stables
near.

There were three or four buggies under cover, but no horses at all, they were farther afield. Across the paddock they went, and up the hill. Half a dozen answered Mr. Hassal's strange whistle; the others were wild, unbroken things, that tossed their manes and fled away at the sight of people to the farthermost parts where the trees grew.

Pip chose one, a grey, with long, fleet-looking legs and a narrow, beautiful head; he prided himself upon knowing something about "points." Judy picked a black, with reddish, restless eyes, but Mr. Hassal refused it because it had an uncertain temper, so she had to be content with a brown with a soft, satiny nose.

Meg asked for "something very quiet" in a whisper Judy and Pip could not hear, and was given a buggy horse that had carried Mrs. Hassal eighteen years ago. Each animal was to be at the complete disposal of the young people during their stay at Yarrahappini, but the rides would have to take place before breakfast or after tea, they were told, if they wanted any pleasure out of them; the rest of the day was unbearable on horseback. Nellie was disappointed in the sheep, exceedingly so. She had expected to find great snow-white beautiful creatures that would be tame and allow her to put ribbon on their necks and lead them about.

From the hill-top the second morning she saw paddock after paddock, each with a brown, slowly moving mass; she ran down through the sunshine with Bunty to view them more closely.

"Oh, *what* a shame!" she exclaimed, actual tears

of disappointment springing to her eyes when she saw the great fat things with their long, dirty, ragged-looking fleece.

"Wait for a time, little woman," Mr. Hassal said; "just you wait till we give them their baths."

CHAPTER 17

Cattle-Drafting at Yarrahappini

"To wheel the wild scrub cattle at the yard,
With a running fire of stockwhip and a fiery run of hoofs."

PIP COULD HARDLY SLEEP ONE NIGHT, a
month after their arrival, for thinking of the cattle-
drafting that was on the programme for the morrow.
He had been casting about for some fresh occupa-
tion, for he was a boy to whom variety was the salt
of life. At first he had been certain he could never
tire of shooting rabbits. Mr. Hassal had given him
the "jolliest little stunner of a gun," and Tettawonga had gone out with him the first day, and had
been very scornful about his enthusiasm when he
shot two.

" Ba' al good, gun do. Plenty fellow rabbit longa
scrub, budgery way north, budgery way south, budgery way eblywhere. Ba' al good barbed wire fence
do, ba' al good poison do. Bah! "

But Pip was not to be discouraged, and really
thought he had done great good to the Yarrahappini
estate by shooting those two soft, fleet brown things.
He took them home and displayed them proudly to

153

the girls, cleaned his perfectly clean gun, and sallied forth the next day.

Tettawonga took his pipe from between his lips when he saw him again and laughed, a loud cackling laugh, that made Pip flush with anger.

"Kimbriki and kimbriki, too! Rabbit he catti, curri-curri now. Boy come long with cawbawn gun, rabbit jerund drekaly, go burri, grass grow, sheep get fat—ha, ha, he, he!"[1]

Pip understood his mixed English enough to know he was making fun of him, and told him wrathfully to "shut up for a Dutch idiot."

Then he shouldered the gun he was so immeasurably proud of and went off the other side of the barbed-wire fence, where was the happy hunting-ground of the little rodent that would not allow Mr. Hassal to grow rich.

He shot five that day, four the next, seven the next, but after a time he voted it slow, and went after gill birds, with more enjoyment but less certainty of a bag.

Every day was filled to the brim with enjoyment, and but for the intense heat that first month at Yarrahappini would have been one of absolute content and happiness.

And now there was the cattle-drafting!

Breakfast was very early the morning of the great event; by half-past five it was almost over, and Pip, in a fever of restlessness, was telling Mr. Hassal he was sure they would be late and miss it.

---

[1] "To-morrow and to-morrow too! Rabbit, he go away quickly now. Boy come along with big gun, rabbit he afraid directly, go under the ground."

Judy had pleaded hard to be allowed to go, but everyone said it was out of the question—indeed, it was doubted if it were wise to allow Pip to face the danger that is inseparable with the drafting of the wilder kind of cattle that had been driven from great distances.

But he had forcibly carried the day, and dressed himself up in so business-like a way that Mr. Hassel had not the heart to refuse him. He came down to breakfast in a Crimean shirt and a pair of old serge trousers fastened round the waist with a leathern belt, in which an unsheathed bowie knife, freshly sharpened, was jauntily stuck. No persuasions would induce him either to wear a coat or sheathe the knife.

The grey was brought round to the veranda steps, with Mr. Hassal's own splendid horse. Mr. Gillet was there on a well-groomed roan; he had three stock-whips, two quite sixteen feet long, the third a shorter one, which he presented to Pip.

The boy's face glowed. "Hurrah, Fizz!" he said, standing up in his saddle and brandishing it round his head. "What 'ud you give to change places?"

He dug his heels into the animal's sides and went helter-skelter at a wild gallop down the hill.

It was a mile and a half to the cattle yards, and there was the strongest excitement.

Pip could not think where all the men had sprung from. There were some twenty or thirty of them, stockmen, shearers "on the wallaby," as their parlance expressed lack of employment, two aboriginals, exclusive of Tettawonga, who was smoking and looking on with sleepy enjoyment, and several other of the station hands.

In the first yard there were five hundred cattle that had been driven there the night before, and that just now presented the appearance of a sea of wildly lashing tails and horns. Such horns! —great, branching, terrific-looking things that they gored and fought each other madly with, seeing they could not get to the common enemy outside.

Just for the first moment or two Pip felt a little disinclined to quit the stronghold of his horse's back. The thunder of hoofs and horns, the wild charges made by the desperate animals against the fence, made him expect to see it come crashing down every minute.

But everybody else had gone to "cockatoo"—to sit on the top rail of the enclosure and look down at the maddened creatures, so at length he fastened his bridle to a tree and proceeded gingerly to follow their example.

At a sudden signal from Mr. Hassal the men dropped down inside, half along one side and half the other. The object was to get a hundred or two of the cattle into the forcing-yard adjoining, the gate to which was wide open. Pip marvelled at the courage of the men; for a moment his heart had leaped to his mouth as bullock after bullock essayed to charge them, but the air resounded with cracks from the mighty stockwhips and drafting-sticks, and beast after beast retreated towards the centre with its face dripping with blood.

Then one huge black creature, with a bellow that seemed to shake the plain, made a wild rush to the gate, the whole herd at his heels. Like lightning, the men made a line behind, shouting, yelling, cracking their whips to drive them onward. Pip stood up and halloed, absolutely beside himself with excitement. Then he held his breath again.

Mr. Hassal and one of the black boys were creeping cautiously up near the gateway through which the tumultuous stream of horns and backs was pouring. Half a dozen mighty blows from the men, and the last leader fell back for an instant, driving the multitude back behind him.

In that second the two had slipped up the rails and the herd was in two divisions.

Two lines of stockmen again, whip-crackings, bellows, blood, horns, hide and heels in the air, and some forty or fifty were secure in a third yard, a long narrow place with a gate at the end leading into the final division.

Pip learnt from Mr. Gillet the object of these divisions: some of the beasts were almost worthless things, and had been assigned to a buyer for a couple of pounds a head, just for the horns, hides, and what might be got for the flesh. Others were prime, fat creatures, ready for the butcher and Sydney market. And others again were splendid animals, of great value for prize and breeding purposes, and were to be made into a separate draft.

The man at the last gateway was doing the all-important work of selecting. He was armed with a short thick stick, and, as the other men drove the animals down towards him, decided with lightning speed to which class they belonged. A heavy blow on the nose, a sharp, rapid series of them between the eyes, and the most violent brute plunged blindly whither the driver sent him. All the day work went on, and just as the great hot purple shadows began to fall across the plain they secured the last rail, the battle was over, and the animals in approved divisions.

Pip ate enough salt beef and damper to half kill him, drank more tea than he had ever disposed of at one sitting in all his fourteen years, swung himself into his saddle in close imitation of the oldest stock-man, and thought if he only could have a black, evil-looking pipe like Tettawonga and the rest of the men his happiness would be complete and his manhood attained.

He reached home as tired as "a dozen dogs and a dingo," and entertained his sisters and Bunty with a graphic account of the day's proceedings, dwelling lengthily on his own prowess and the manifold perils he had escaped.

The next day both Esther and Judy rode with the others to the yards to see the departures.

The best of the contingent, which Mr. Hassal had only wanted to separate, not to sell, were driven out through the gate and away to their old fields and pastures stale.

The "wasters," some hundred and fifty of them, with half a dozen stockmen mounted on the best horses of the place told off for them, were released from their enclosure in a state of frenzied despera-tion, and, with much cracking of whips and yells, mustered into a herd and driven across the plain in the direction of the road. And some hour or two later the best "beef" lot were driven forth, and quiet reigned at Yarrahappini once more.

During the two days of excitement the children all decided upon their future professions, which were all to be of a pastoral nature.

Pip was going to be a stockman, and brand and draft cattle all the days of his life. Judy was going to be his *aide-de-camp*, provided he let her stay in the saddle, and provided her with a whip just as long as his own. Meg thought she should like to marry the richest squatter in Australia, and have the Governor and the Premier come up for shooting and "things," and give balls to which all the people within a hundred miles would come. Nell decided she would make soap and candles, coloured as well as plain, when she arrived at years of discretion; and Baby inclined to keeping paddocks full of pet lambs that never grew into sheep.

Bunty did not wax enthusiastic over any of the ideas.

"I'd rather be like Mr. Gillet," he said, and his eyes looked dreamy.

"Pooh! no books and figures for me; give me a run of Salt Bush country, and a few thousand sheep," said Pip.

"Hear! hear! " chimed in Judy.

"Stoopids!" said Bunty, in a voice of great scorn. "Doesn't Mr. Gillet keep the store keys—just *think* of those currants and figs."

CHAPTER 18

The Picnic at Krangi-Bahtoo

ESTHER HAD GONE TO A BALL, not in a
dress of delicate colour with great puffed sleeves,
and a dazzling neck bare and beautiful under its
wraps, not through the darkness to a blaze of lights
and swinging music.

She had gone, in the broad light of the morning,
in a holland suit with a blue Henley shirt, a sailor
hat, and a gossamer.

Under the front buggy seat where Mr. Hassal sat
was a box containing a beautiful gown, all daffodil
silk and delicate wavelets of chiffon. And there were
daffodil shoes and stockings, a plume fan in a
hat-box on her knee, and a lovely trained white
underskirt with billowy frills of torchon, the
very sight of which made Meg wild to be grown
up.

But none of these things were to be donned for
many an hour yet.

The ball was a neat little matter of fifty-five miles
away, across country, so she had to start tolerably
early, of course, in order to have comfortable time
to " titivate," as Pip expressed it.

The children, as compensation for having no part

in this pleasure, were to have a very out-of-the-way
kind of picnic all to themselves.

In the first place, the picnic ground was fourteen
miles away; in the second, the journey was to be
made, not in everyday buggies, or on commonplace
horses, but on a dray drawn by a team of twelve
yoked bullocks.

A boundary-rider had reported that a magnificent
blue gum that they had long called King Koree had
been blown down during a violent gale, and Mr.
Hassal immediately declared that, whatever the
trouble, it must be brought for the foundation of a
kind of dam across the creek at Krangi-Bahtoo, the
picnic spot. The fallen bush monarch lay twenty
miles away from the station, and six beyond the
place chosen for the picnic; so it was arranged the
trolly should carry the party for the fourteen miles,
leave them to picnic, go forward for the tree, bring
it back, and deposit it near the creek ready for
future operations, and bring the children back in
the cool of the evening.

But for escorting his daughter to the ball, Mr.
Hassal would have gone himself to the place and
seen about it in person. As it was, he placed the
great trolly in the charge of four men, with instruc-
tions to pick up a couple of men from distant huts
to help in the task.

Krangi-Bahtoo—or Duck Water, as, less prettily,
we should call it—was the name given to the head
of the creek, which had scooped out the earth till
it made itself a beautiful ravine just there, with
precipitous rocks and boulders that the kangaroos
skipped across and played hide-and-seek behind

with hunters, and great towering blue gums and red gums, that seemed to lose themselves in the blue, blue sky-canopy above.

Tettawonga told of a Bunyip that dwelt where the trickling water had made a pool, deep and beautiful, and delicate ferns had crept tenderly to fringe its edge, and blackwood, and ti-trees grown up thick and strong for a girdle. The water-hen made a home there, the black swan built among the grass-like reeds, the wild duck made frequent dark zigzag lines against the sky. From the trees the bell-bird, the coach-whip, the tewinga, the laughing-jackass, the rifle-bird and regent, filled the air with sound, if not with music. And the black snake, the brown snake, the whip, the diamond, and the death adder glided gently among the fallen leaves and grasses, and held themselves in cheerful readiness for intruders. That was why a condition was attached to the freely granted picnic.

Everyone might go, and go on the bullock-dray, but the picnic was to take place above the ravine, and no one was to venture down, on pain of being instantly packed back to Sydney.

They all promised faithfully. Mrs. Hassal, tiny as she was, had a way of commanding implicit obedience.

Then an incredible number of hampers, brimming over with good things, was packed.

Mr. Gillet went, to give an appearance of steadiness to the party, and to see no one got sunstroke.

He had a Heine in one pocket against the long, unusual day, a bulging Tennyson in the other, and a sheaf of English papers under his arm as he climbed on the trolly, where the whole seven were already seated.

The *seven?* Even so.

Judy had refused to stir without the General, and had promised "on her life" not to allow any harm to come near him.

Mr. Gillet gave a glance almost of dismay when he found the whole number was to be present, without the subtraction of the mischievously disposed ones, or the addition of anyone but himself weighted with authority. For a moment he distrusted his own powers in such a situation.

Judy caught the doubting look.

"You're quoting poetry to yourself, Mr. Gillet," she said.

"I?" he said, and looked astonished. "Indeed, no. What makes you think so, Miss Judy?"

"I can hear it distinctly," she said. "Your eyes are saying it, and your left ear, not to mention the ends of your moustache."

"Judy!" reproved Meg, whom something had made strangely quiet.

He pretended to be alarmed—shut his eyes, held his left ear, covered his moustache.

"What can they be saying?" he said.

> "'Oh that I was where I would be!
> Then I would be where I am not:
> But where I am I still must be,
> And where I would be I cannot.'

Meg, I *wish* you would stop treading on my toes."

So after that even Mr. Gillet grew gay and talkative, to show he was enjoying himself, and the

163

bullocks caught the infection of the brimming spirits behind them, and moved a *leetle* bit faster than snails. When they had crept along over about ten miles, however, the slow motion and the heat that beat down sobered them a little.

"Miss Meg, that silver-grey gum before you, guileless of leaves, indicates Duck Water."

How glad they were to unfold themselves and stretch out their arms and legs on the ground at last. No one had dreamt riding behind a bullock team could have been so "flat, stale, and unprofitable," as it was after the first mile or two.

Then the trolly continued its course.

"I doubt if they will be back before the sun goes down, if they don't go a little quicker," Mr. Gillet said; "it is lunch-time now."

They were in a great grassed paddock that at one end fell abruptly down to the ravine and swamp lands known as "Duck Water."

A belt of great trees made a shade at one side, and along the other was the barbed-wire fence that showed they had not got away from the Yarrahappini estate even yet: higher up was the lonely bark hut of one of the stockmen.

They went up in a body to speak to him before he joined the bullock team, and to view his solitary dwelling.

Just a small room it was, with a wide fireplace and chimney, where hung a frying-pan, a billy, a cup, and a spoon. There was a bunk in one corner, with a couple of blue blankets on it, a deal table and one chair in the middle of the room. Over the fire-place hung a rough cupboard, made out of a soap-box, and

164

used to hold rations. From a nail in the low ceiling a mosquito-net bag was suspended, and the buzzing flies around proclaimed that it held meat. The walls were papered with many a copy of *The Illustrated Sydney News*, and *The Town and Country Journal*; there was a month-old *Daily Telegraph* lying on the chair, where the owner had laid it down.

A study in brown the stockman was: brown, dull eyes; brown, dusty-looking hair; brown skin, sun-dried and shrivelled; brown, unkempt beard; brown trousers of corduroy, and brown coat.

His pipe was black, however—a clay, that looked as if it had been smoked for twenty years.

"Wouldn't you like to be nearer the homestead?" Meg asked. "Isn't it lonely?"

"Not ter mention," the brown man said to his pipe or his beard.

"What do you do with yourself when you're not outside?" asked Pip.

"Smoke," said the man.

"But on Sundays, and all through the evenings?"

"Smoke," he said.

"On Cwismas day," Baby said, pressing to see this strange man; "zen what does you do?"

"Smoke," he said.

Judy wanted to know how long he'd lived in the little place, and everyone was stricken dumb to hear he had been there most of the time for seven years.

"Don't you ever forget how to talk?" she said, in an awestruck voice.

But he answered laconically to his beard that there was the cat.

Baby had found it already under the kerosene tin

that did duty for a bucket, and it had scratched her in three places: brown, like its master, it was evil-eyed, fiercely whiskered, thin as a rail; still, there was the affection of years between the two.

Mr. Gillet told him of the squatter's wish that he should go with the other men and help with the tree.

He pulled a brown hat over his brow and moved away towards the bullock-dray, which had crept up the winding road by now to the hill-top.

"Water in tub, nearer than creek," he muttered to his pipe before he went, and they found his tub-tank and gladly filled the billy ready for lunch.

Mrs. Hassal's roast fowls and duck tasted well, even though they frizzled on the plates as if the sun were trying to finish their cooking. And the apple tarts and apricot turnovers vanished speedily; and of the fruit salad that came forth from two screw-top bottles, not a teaspoonful remained to tell a tale.

Mr. Gillet had brought materials for a damper, by special request, and after lunch prepared to make it, so they might have it for afternoon tea.

"Pheough!" said Judy. "Is *that* how you make it? You need not give *me* any."

It certainly was manufactured with surprising celerity.

Mr. Gillet merely tossed some flour from a bag out upon a plate, added a pinch of salt and some water; then he shaped it into a cake of dough, and laid it on the ashes of the fire, covering it all over with the hot, silver ash.

"*How* dirty!" said Nell, elevating her pretty little nose.

But when it was cooked, and Mr. Gillet lifted it up and dusted the ash away—lo! it was high and light and beautifully white.

So they ate it, and took mental marginal notes to make it in the paddocks at Misrule for each and every picnic to come.

They piled up two plates of good things and put in the brown man's cupboard, and Mr. Gillet laid his unread English papers on the chair near the cat.

"That *Telegraph* is a month old," he said deprecatingly, seeing Meg smile upon him her first smile that day.

CHAPTER 19

A Pale-Blue Hair Ribbon

*"She in her virginal beauty
As pure as a pictured saint,
How should this sinning and sorrow
Have for her danger or taint?"*

THE REASON OUR SWEET PALE MARGARET
had been reluctant of her smiles was on account of
the very man who alone missed them.

Quite a warm friendship had sprung up during
the month between the little fair-faced girl, who
looked with such serene blue eyes to a future she
felt must be beautiful, and the world-worn man,
who looked back to a past all blackened and unlovely
by his own acts.

He rode with the two girls every day, because
Mrs. Hassal did not like them going long distances
alone; and, seeing Judy seldom walked her horse,
and Meg's steed had not a canter in it, it fell out
that he kept beside the slow and timid rider all the
time.

"You remind me of a little sister I had who
died," he said slowly to Meg once, after a long talk.
"Perhaps if she were alive now I should not be
quite so contemptible."

168

Meg's face flushed scarlet, and a shamed look had come into her eyes. It seemed altogether terrible to her that he should know she knew of his failing.

"Perhaps it makes her sorry now," she said in a whisper he scarcely heard, and then she grew pale at her boldness, and rode on a little way to hide her distressed looks.

On the way home the pale-blue ribbon, that tied the strands of her sunny plait together, blew off. He dismounted and picked it up. Meg stretched out her hand for it, but he untied the bow and folded it slowly round his big hand.

"May I keep it?" he said in a low voice. "For my blue ribbon? I know the conditions that attach."

"If you would—oh, *if* you would!" Meg breathed rather than said. Then Judy galloped up and they rode home three abreast. It was such happiness to her all the hot, long days that followed; to a girl just entering life there can be no purer, deeper feeling of pleasure than that brought by the knowledge that she is influencing for good some man or woman older than herself, more sin-worn and earth-wearied. Poor little Meg! Her tender rose dreams had pictured her big *protégé* a man among men again, holding up his head once more, taking his place in the world, going back to the old country and claiming the noble lady her fertile imagination had pictured waiting so patiently for him; and all this because she, Meg Woolcot, had stepped into his life and pointed the way he should go.

And then she went to swing in a hammock on

the back veranda, and all her castles came tumbling about her ears, dealing her sharp, bitter blows.

There was a thick creeper of passion-fruit vines behind her, and through it she could hear Tettawonga talking to the cook.

" Marse Gillet on the burst agen," he said, and chuckled through the side of his lips where his pipe did not rest.

Meg sat up in horror. Since she had been at Yarrahappini she had heard the phrase applied to too many of the station hands not to know that it meant a reckless drinking bout.

" Lor'! *I'm* not surprised," the woman said, " he's been too sober late days to keep it up; s'pose he's been trying to last the visitors out, but found it too much. Who's got the keys? "

" Mis' Hassal," he said, " you to helpin' her—ba' al good for stores to-day, Marse Gillet—he, he, ha, ha! "

So that was what had happened to him all these three days she had not seen him! She had heard he had ridden over to the next station on business for Mr. Hassal, but had not dreamed such a thing had overtaken him. The fifth day she had seen him in the distance, once coming out of the storeroom and looking exactly like himself, only his shoulders stooped a little more, and once smoking outside his own door.

The sixth day was the picnic.

Just as light-hearted and merry as the others she could not feel, with this disappointment at her heart, this shaken trust in human nature.

How weak he was, she thought, how ignoble!

All her pity was swept away in a young, large indignation.

She had hardly shaken hands when they had met in the morning, and all the long drive she was persistently cold towards him.

After lunch the party became scattered. Judy took the General and went over to the belt of trees; Pip and Bunty occupied themselves with catching locusts; Baby and Nell gathered wild flowers. Meg knelt down to collect the spoons and forks and put the untouched food back into the baskets away from the ants.

" I will do this—you look hot, Miss Meg; sit down quietly," Mr. Gillet said.

"Thank you, but I prefer to do it myself," Miss Meg said, with freezing dignity.

She did not look at him, but there was a certain tightness about her lips that made him know the light in her clear young eyes was a scornful one.

He did not offer again, but sat and watched her pack up the things with an untranslatable look on his face. When she had almost finished he took something out of his pocket.

"I have to give you this again," he said, and handed her the blue length of ribbon, folded smoothly, but showing the crease where it had been tied.

She took it without lifting her eyes, crushed it up in her hand, and slipped it into her pocket.

"I had almost hoped you would say I might keep it, in spite of everything," he said, "just as a talisman against the future, but your lips are too

171

severe, Miss Meg, for me to cherish the hope any longer."

"It would be as useless as it has been," she said stiffly. Her hands moved nervously, however, and she wrapped up the remains of a duck and a jam tart together.

"Then I am not to have another chance?" he said.

"It would be no use," Meg repeated, gathering up bananas and oranges with a heightened colour.

He does not realize how wicked he has been, he thinks he ought to be forgiven at once, was her thought.

He emptied the billy slowly on the ground, he put on its blackened lid and tied the newspaper around it. Then he looked at her again, and the way her soft hair fell on her forehead made him think of his young dead sister.

"I *beg* you to give it to me again, little Miss Meg," he said.

Meg's heart and head had a rapid battle; the former was tender and charitable, and bade her take the little ribbon and give it to him instantly; the latter said he had sinned greatly, and she must show him her disapproval by her manner, even if she yielded what he asked her in the end. The head won.

"My influence is evidently useless—that bit of ribbon would make no difference in the future," she said very coldly.

He leaned back against the tree and yawned, as if the subject had no more interest for him.

172

"Ah well," he said, "I dare say you are right."

Meg felt a little taken down.

"Of course, if you really want the ribbon you can have it," she said loftily. She took it from her pocket and tendered it to him.

But he made no effort to take it.

"Keep it to tie your hair again, little girl," he said; "after all, I don't suppose it would be any use."

Meg continued her packing with burning cheeks, and he filled up his pipe and smoked it, watching her idly the while.

"It's an odd thing," he said, more as if making an observation than addressing her, "but the gentlest-looking women are nearly always the hardest."

Meg opened her mouth to speak, but found nothing to say, so closed it again and began to count Mrs. Hassal's forks for the fourth time.

"I wonder would you mind if I gave you a little advice, Miss Meg, in return for all you have given me," he said, taking his pipe from his mouth and looking at it as if he were trying to find out the lettering on its nickel plate.

"Certainly not."

She laid down the bundle and looked at him with calm, surprised eyes. "Say whatever you please, I do not mind in the very least."

He sat up and played with the handle of a strap while he spoke.

"You have brothers," he said; "some day they will go a little astray—for it is only women like you, Miss Meg, and angels who can keep to the path always. Don't be too hard on them. Don't make an effort to show them the difference between your whiteness and their blackness. They will see it right enough, but they won't like you to draw their attention to it. Try and look gentle and forgiving —they'll feel quite as miserable as you could wish them to feel. The world has a beautiful frown of its own, and an endless vocabulary of cold words— wouldn't it do if the little sisters left it the monopoly of them?"

"Oh-h-h!" said Meg. Her cheeks were crimson, and all the dignity had oozed out of her voice.

He buckled the strap round nothing with infinite care, and went on again in a low tone:

"Suppose Pip did something very wrong some day, and the world flung stones at him till he was bruised all over. And suppose, feeling very wretched, he came home to his sisters. And Meg, because wickedness was abhorrent to her, threw a few more little stones, so that the pain might teach him a lesson he could not forget. And Judy, because he was her brother and in trouble, flung her arms round him and encouraged him, and helped him to fight the world again, and gave him never a hard word or look, thinking he had had plenty. Which sister's influence would be greater, Miss Meg?"

Meg's little soft mouth was quivering, her eyes were on the ground, because the tears would have splashed out if she had lifted them.

"Oh-h-h!" she said again. "Oh, how very horrid I have been—oh-h-h!"

She covered her face with her hands, for one of the quickly gathered tears was trembling on her lashes.

Mr. Gillet dropped the strap and the pipe, and looked across to her with tender eyes.

"I am more than twice your age, Miss Meg, old enough nearly to be your father—you will forgive me for saying all this, won't you? I was thinking of my sister who died. I had another little sister, too, a year older, but she was hard—I only went to her once. She is one of the best women in England now, but her lips are severe. Little Miss Meg, I could not bear the thought of you growing hard."

Half a dozen big tears had fallen down among the forks. Meg was crying because it was borne upon her what a very hateful creature she was. First Alan lectured her and spoke of his sister, and now this man.

He misinterpreted her silence.

"I have no right to speak to you like this, because my life has been any colour but white—that is it, isn't it, Miss Meg?" he said with great sadness.

Meg dropped her sheltering hands.

"Oh, no," she said, "oh! how *can* you think so? It is only I am so horrid." She rummaged in her pocket and brought out the ribbon.

"Will you take it again?" she said—"oh, *please*, just to make me feel less horrid. Oh, please take it!"

She looked at him with wet, imploring eyes, and held it out.

He took it, smoothed its crumpledness, and placed it in his pocket-book.

"God bless you," he said, and the tone made Meg sob.

CHAPTER 20

Little Judy

ACROSS THE GRASS came a little flying figure, Judy in a short pink frock with her wild curls blowing about her face.

"Are you a candidate for sunstroke—where *is* your hat, Miss Judy?" Mr. Gillet asked.

Judy shook back her dark tangle.

"Sorrow a know I knows," she said—"it's a banana the General is afther dyin' for, and sure it's a dead body I shall live to see misself if you've eaten all the oranges."

Meg pushed the bag of fruit across the cloth to her, and tried to tilt her hat over her tell-tale eyes.

But the bright dark ones had seen the wet lashes the first moment.

"I s'pose you've been reading stupid poetry and making Meg cry?" she said, with an aggressive glance from Mr. Gillet to the book on the grass. "You really ought to be ashamed of yourselves, *sich* behaviour at a picnic. It's been a saving in oranges though, that's a mercy."

She took half a dozen great fat ones from the bag, as well as four or five bananas, and went back with

M 177

flying steps to the belt of trees, where the General in his holland coat could just be seen.

He was calmly grubbing up the earth and putting it in his little red mouth when she arrived with the bananas.

He looked up at her with an adorable smile.

" *Baby!* " she said, swooping down upon him with one of her wild rushes—" *baby!* "

She kissed him fifty times; it almost hurt her sometimes, the feeling of love for this little fat, dirty boy.

Then she gathered him up on her knee and wiped as much of the dirt as possible from his mouth with the corner of his coat.

" Narna," he said, struggling on to the ground again; so she took the skin from a great yellow one and put it in his small, chubby hand.

He ate some of it, and squeezed the rest up tightly in his hands, gleefully watching it come up between his wee fingers in little worm-like morsels.

Then he smeared it over his dimpled face, and even rubbed it on his hair, while Judy was engrossed with her fifth orange.

So, of course, she had to whip him for doing it, or pretend to, which came to the same thing. And then he had to whip her, which did not only mean pretence.

He beat her with a stick he found near, he smacked her face and pulled her hair and bumped himself up and down on her chest, and all in such solemn, painstaking earnestness that she could only laugh even when he really hurt her.

" Dood now? " he said at last anxiously. And she

began to weep noisily, with covered face and shaking shoulders, in the proper, penitent way. And then he put his darling arms round her neck and hugged her, and said " Ju-Ju " in a choking little voice, and patted her cheeks, and gave her a hundred eager, wide, wet kisses till she was better.

Then they played chasings, and the General fell down twenty times, and scratched his little knees and hands, and struggled up again and staggered on.

Presently Judy stood still in a hurry; there was a tick working its slow way into her wrist. Only its two back legs were left out from under the skin, and for a long time she pulled and pulled without any success. Then it broke in two, and she had to leave one half in for little Grandma and kerosene to extract on their return.

Two or three minutes it had taken her to try to move it, and when she looked up the General had toddled some distance away, and was travelling along as fast as ever his little fat legs would carry him, thinking he was racing her. Just as she started after him he looked back, his eyes dancing, his face dimpled and mischievous, and, oh! so dirty.

And then—ah, God!

It is so hard to write it. My pen has had only happy writing to do so far, and now!

"You rogue!" Judy called, pretending to run very quickly. Then the whole world seemed to rise up before her.

There was a tree falling, one of the great, gaunt, naked things that had been ringbarked long ago. All day it had swayed to and fro, rotten through and through; now there came up across the plain a puff of wind, and down it went before it. One wild ringing cry Judy gave, then she leaped across the ground, her arms outstretched to the little lad running with laughing eyes and lips straight to death.

The crash shook the trees around, the very air seemed splintered.

They had heard it—all the others—heard the wild cry and then the horrible thud.

How their knees shook! what blanched faces they had as they rushed towards the sound!

They lifted it off the little bodies—the long, silvered trunk with the gum dead and dried in streaks upon it. Judy was face downwards, her arms spread out.

And underneath her was the General, a little shaken, mightily astonished, but quite unhurt.

Meg clasped him for a minute, but then laid him down, and gathered with the others close around Judy.

Oh, the little dark, quiet head, the motionless body, in its pink, crushed frock, the small, thin, outspread hands!

"Judy!" Pip said, in a voice of beseeching agony.

But the only answer was the wind at the tree-tops and the frightened breathings of the others.

Mr. Gillet remembered there was no one to act but himself. He went with Pip to the stockman's hut, and they took the door off its leather hinges and carried it down the hill.

"I will lift her," he said, and passed his arms around the little figure, raising her slowly, slowly, gently upwards, laying her on the door with her face to the sky.

But she moaned—oh, how she moaned!

Pip, whose heart had leapt to his throat at the first sign of life, almost went mad as the little sounds of agony burst from her lips.

They raised the stretcher, and bore her up the hill to the little brown hut at the top.

Then Mr. Gillet spoke, outside the doorway, to Meg and Pip, who seemed dazed, stunned.

"It will be hours before we can get help, and it is five now," he said. "Pip, there is a doctor staying at Boolagri, ten miles along the road. Fetch him—run all the way. I will go back home—fourteen miles. Miss Meg, I can't be back all at once. I will bring a buggy; the bullock-dray is too slow and jolting, even when it comes back. You must watch by her, give her water if she asks—there is nothing else you can do."

"She is dying?" Meg said—"dying?"

He thought of all that might happen before he brought help, and dare not leave her unprepared.

"I think her back is broken," he said, very quietly. "If it is, it means death."

Pip fled away down the road that led to the doctor's.

Mr. Gillet gave a direction or two, then he looked at Meg.

"Everything depends on you; you must not even think of breaking down," he said. "Don't move her, watch all the time."

He moved away towards the lower road.

She sprang after him.

"Will she die while you are away?—no one but me."

Her eyes were wild, terrified.

"God knows!" he said, and turned away.

It was almost more than he could bear to go and leave this little girl alone to face so terrible a thing.

"God help me!" she moaned, hurrying back, but not looking at the hot, low-hanging sky. "Help me, God! God, help me, help me!"

CHAPTER 21

When the Sun Went Down

SUCH A SUNSET!

Down at the foot of the grass hill there was a flame-coloured sky, with purple, soft clouds massed in banks high up where the dying glory met the paling blue. The belt of trees had grown black, and stretched sombre, motionless arms against the orange background. All the wind had died, and the air hung hot and still, freighted with the strange silence of the bush.

And at the top of the hill, just within the doorway of the little brown hut, her wide eyes on the wonderful heavens, Judy lay dying. She was very quiet now, though she had been talking—talking of all sorts of things. She told them she had no pain at all.

"Only I shall die when they move me," she said.

Meg was sitting in a little heap on the floor beside her. She had never moved her eyes from the face on the pillow of mackintoshes, she had never opened her white lips to say one word.

Outside the bullocks stood motionless against the sky—Judy said they looked like stuffed ones having their portrait taken. She smiled the least little bit, but Meg said, "Don't," and writhed.

Two of the men had gone on superfluous errands for help; the others stood some distance away, talking in subdued voices.

There was nothing for them to do. The brown man had been talking—a rare thing for him.

He had soothed the General off to sleep, and laid him in the bunk with the blue blanket tucked around him. And he had made a billy of hot, strong tea, and asked the children, with tears in his eyes, to drink some, but none of them would.

Baby had fallen to sleep on the floor, her arms clasped tightly around Judy's lace-up boot.

Bunty was standing, with a stunned look on his white face, behind the stretcher. His eyes were on his sister's hair, but he did not dare to let them wander to her face, for fear of what he should see there. Nellie was moving all the time—now to the fence to strain her eyes down the road, where the evening shadows lay heavily, now to fling herself face downward behind the hut and say, "Make her better, God! God, make her better, make her better! Oh! *can't* You make her better?"

Greyer grew the shadows round the little hut, the bullocks' outlines had faded, and only an indistinct mass of soft black loomed across the light. Behind the trees the fire was going out, here and there were yellow, vivid streaks yet, but the flaming sun-edge had dipped beyond the world, and the purple, delicate veil was dropping down.

A curlew's note broke the silence, wild, mournful,

unearthly. Meg shivered, and sat up straight. Judy's brow grew damp, her eyes dilated, her lips trembled.

"Meg!" she said, in a whisper that cut the air. "Oh, Meg, I'm frightened! *Meg*, I'm so frightened!"

"God!" said Meg's heart.

"Meg, say something. Meg, help me! Look at the dark, Meg. *Meg*, I can't die! Oh, why don't they be quick?"

Nellie flew to the fence again; then to say, "Make her better, God—oh, please, God!"

"Meg, I can't think of anything to say. Can't you say something, Meg? Aren't there any prayers about the dying in the Prayer Book?—I forget. Say something, Meg!"

Meg's lips moved, but her tongue uttered no word.

"Meg, I'm so frightened! I can't think of anything but 'For what we are about to receive,' and that's grace, isn't it? And there's nothing in Our Father that would do either. Meg, I wish we'd gone to Sunday school and learnt things. Look at the dark, Meg! Oh, Meg, hold my hands!"

"Heaven won't—be—dark," Meg's lips said.

Even when speech came, it was only a halting, stereotyped phrase that fell from them.

"If it's all gold and diamonds, I don't want to go!" The child was crying now. "Oh, Meg, I want to be alive! How'd you like to die, Meg, when you're only thirteen? Think how lonely I'll be without you all. Oh, Meg! Oh, Pip, Pip! Oh, Baby! Nell!"

The tears streamed down her cheeks, her chest rose and fell.

"Oh, say something, Meg!—hymns!—anything!"

Half the book of *Hymns Ancient and Modern* danced across Meg's brain. Which one could she think of that would bring quiet into those feverish eyes that were fastened on her face with such a frightening, imploring look?

Then she opened her lips:

> "Come unto Me, ye weary,
>   And I will give you rest,
>   Oh, bl——"

"I'm not weary, I don't *want* to rest," Judy said, in a fretful tone.

Again Meg tried:

> "My God, my Father, while I stray
>   Far from my home on life's rough way,
>   Oh, teach me from my heart to say—
>   Thy will be done!"

"That's for old people," said the little tired voice. "He won't expect *me* to say it."

Then Meg remembered the most beautiful hymn in the world, and said the first and last verses without a break in her voice:

> "Abide with me, fast falls the eventide,
>   The darkness deepens; Lord, with me abide.
>   When other helpers fail, and comforts flee,
>   Help of the helpless, oh, abide with me!

Hold Thou Thy Cross before my closing eyes,
Shine through the gloom and point me to the skies.
Heaven's morning breaks, and earth's vain shadows
flee
In life, in death, O Lord, abide with me!

"Oh! and Judy, dear, we are forgetting; there's Mother, Judy, dear—you won't be lonely! Can't you remember Mother's eyes, little Judy?"

Judy grew quiet, and still more quiet. She shut her eyes so she could not see the gathering shadows.

Meg's arms were round her, Meg's cheek was on her brow, Nell was holding her hands, Baby her feet, Bunty's lips were on her hair. Like that they went with her right to the Great Valley, where there are no lights even for stumbling, childish feet.

The shadows were cold, and smote upon their hearts; they could feel the wind from the strange waters on their brows; but only she who was about to cross heard the low lapping of the waves.

Just as her feet touched the water there was a figure in the doorway.

"Judy!" said a wild voice; and Pip brushed them aside and fell down beside her.

"Judy, Judy, *Judy!*"

The light flickered back in her eyes. She kissed him with pale lips once, twice; she gave him both her hands, and her last smile.

Then the wind blew over them all, and, with a little shudder, she slipped away.

CHAPTER 22

And Last

*"She seemed a thing that could not feel
The touch of earthly years."*

*"No motion has she now — no force;
She neither hears nor sees;
Rolled round in earth's diurnal course,
With rocks and stones and trees."*

THEY WENT HOME AGAIN, the six of them, and Esther, who, all her days, " would go the softlier, sadlier" because of the price that had been paid for the life of her little sweet son. The very air of Yarrahappini seemed to crush them and hang heavy on their souls.

So when the Captain, who had hurried up to see the last of his poor little girl, asked if they would like to go home, they all said "Yes."

There was a green space of ground on a hill-top behind the cottage, and a clump of wattle trees, dark-green now, but gold-crowned and gracious in the spring.

This is where they left little Judy. All around it Mr. Hassal had white tall palings put; the short grave was in the shady corner of it.

The place looked like a tiny churchyard in a

children's country where there had only been one death.

Or a green fair field, with one little garden bed.

Meg was glad the little mound looked to the east; the suns died behind it—the orange and yellow and purple suns she could not bear to watch ever again while she lived.

But away in the east they rose tenderly always, and the light crept up across the sky to the hill-top in delicate pinks and trembling blues and brightening greys, but never fiery, yellow streaks, that made the eyes ache with hot tears.

There was a moon making it white and beautiful when they said good-bye to it on the last day.

They plucked a blade or two of grass each from the fresh turfs, and turned away. Nobody cried; the white stillness of the far moon, the pale, hanging stars, the faint wind stirring the wattles, held back their tears till they had closed the little gate behind them and left her alone on the quiet hill-top.

Then they went back to Misrule, each to pick up the thread of life and go on with the weaving that, thank God, must be done, or hearts would break every day.

Meg had grown older; she would never be quite so young again as she had been before that red sunset sank into her soul.

There was a deeper light in her eyes; such tears as she had wept clear the sight till life becomes a thing more distinct and far-reaching.

Nellie and she went to church the first Sunday after their return. Aldith was a few pews away, light-souled as ever, dressed in gay attire, flashing smiling, coquettish glances across to the Courtneys' pew, and the Grahams sitting just behind.

How far away Meg had grown from her! It seemed years since she had been engrossed with the latest mode in hat trimming, the dip of "umbrella" skirts, and the best method of making the hands white. Years since she had tried a trembling 'prentice hand at flirtations. Years, almost, since she had given the little blue ribbon at Yarrahappini, that was doing more good than she dreamed of.

Alan looked at her from his pew—the little figure in its sorrowful black, the shining hair hanging in a plait no longer frizzed at the end, the chastened droop of the young lips, the wistful sadness of the blue eyes. He could hardly realize it was the little scatterbrain girl who had written that letter, and stolen away through the darkness to meet his graceless young brother.

He clasped her hand when church was over; his grey eyes, with the quick moisture in them, made up for the clumsy, stumbling words of sympathy he tried to speak.

"Let us be friends always, Miss Meg," he said, as they parted at the Misrule gate.

"Yes, let us," said Meg.

And the firm, frank friendship became a beautiful thing in both their lives, strengthening Meg and making the boy gentler.

Pip became his laughing, high-spirited self again, as even the most loving boy will, thanks to the merciful making of young hearts; but he used to get sudden fits of depression at times, and disappear all at once, in the midst of a game of cricket or football, or from the table when the noise was at its highest.

Bunty presented to the world just as grimy a face as of old, and hands even more grubby, for he had taken a mechanical turn of late, and spent his spare moments in manufacturing printing machines—so called—and fearful and wonderful engines, out of an old stove and some pots and rusty frying-pans rescued from the rubbish heap.

But he did not tell quite so many stories in these days; that deep sunset had stolen even into his young heart, and whenever he felt inclined to say " I never, 'twasn't me, 'twasn't my fault," a tangle of dark curls rose before him, just as they had lain that night when he had not dared to move his eyes away from them.

Baby's legs engrossed her very much at present, for she had just been promoted from socks to stockings, and all who remember the occasion in their own lives will realize the importance of it to her.

Nell seemed to grow prettier every day. Pip had his hands full with trying to keep her from growing conceited; if brotherly rubs and snubs availed anything, she ought to have been as lowly minded as if she had had red hair and a nose of heavenward bent.

Esther said she wished she could buy a few extra years, a stern brow, and dignity in large quantities from some place or other—there might be some chance, then, of Misrule resuming its baptismal and unexciting name of The River House.

But, oddly enough, no one echoed the wish.

The Captain never smoked at the end of the side veranda now: the ill-kept lawn made him see always a little figure in a pink frock and battered hat mowing the grass in a blaze of sunlight. Judy's death made his six living children dearer to his heart, though he showed his affection very little more.

The General grew chubbier and more adorable every day he lived. It is no exaggeration to say that they all worshipped him now in his little kingly babyhood, for the dear life had been twice given, and the second time it was Judy's gift, and priceless therefore.

My pen has been moving heavily, slowly, for these last two chapters; it refuses to run lightly, freely again just yet, so I will lay it aside, or I shall sadden you.

Some day, if you would care to hear it, I should like to tell you of my young Australians again, slipping a little space of years.

Until then, farewell and adieu.